# THE DEAD OF WINTER

A MISS RIDDELL AMATEUR FEMALE SLEUTH HISTORICAL COZY MYSTERY

P.C. JAMES

# COPYRIGHT



For more information: email: pj4429358@gmail.com

# 1

## FRIDAY, FEBRUARY 14, 1986

NORTHERN ONTARIO, Canada.

"WHAT MADE Mike invite our precious Miss Riddell?" Joanne Edwards, who preferred to be called Jo, asked Saul Monkhouse, her colleague at Neufeldt and Partners. They were standing together in their boss's lodge looking out into the snowstorm that was just gathering pace. It looked like it was going to be a wild night and Jo's gray eyes widened as the snow swirled before them like a tornado. She was slim, athletic, of medium height, with close-cut dark blonde hair. No Dallas-Dynasty bouffant styles allowed in Jo's focused world, though she did wear the padded shoulder jackets the show had made so popular. No one, not even Jo, was sure if it was her being single that made her so determined for advancement or whether it was her steely focus on advancement that ensured she'd remained single.

Saul shrugged. "He couldn't not invite her, could he? She's our newest recruit. However, dull and serious you and

I find her, she's now one of the team." Saul, like Jo, was a mid-thirties, experienced financial auditor and consultant. They both saw themselves as having a successful future ahead of them and in their eyes the arrival of Pauline Riddell was a hurdle. Saul was also unmarried but, in his case, he knew why. He didn't find anyone attractive in that way; somehow the lust gene that drove everyone else wild, had missed him – and for that, he was thankful. Not finding others attractive didn't mean Saul let himself be unattractive, however. Social conventions, particularly around the business world where he worked so hard to rise, ensured his tall, slim frame kept its shape, and his clothes, suits for work and athletic gear for outside, were selected to complement it. He was fastidious about grooming. No one ever saw Saul with a five o'clock shadow or unkempt hair.

Jo looked around to be sure they weren't being overheard before saying, "I don't see why we needed her at all. She's on the downward side of her career and coming from a failing firm. Seaforth's is almost gone."

Saul nodded. "I hear you," he said. "I know this sounds crazy, but I can't help feeling Mike is sending us a message."

It was Jo's turn to nod. "I wondered about that too." She paused, before adding, "and I wonder what can be done about it."

"Nothing *officially*," Saul said.

"Unofficially, though," Jo continued his thought, "opportunities may come to demonstrate who among us all has the best interests of the firm at heart and the best regard for its reputation."

"I'm sure there will be moments," Saul replied, "where those of us who've put in the graft over the years might be called upon to come to the firm's rescue."

"Teamwork is the key to success in all enterprises," Jo said. "Those who have the best interests of the firm must work together to safeguard its future."

# 2

## WORRYING START

Pauline Riddell drove slowly over the snow drifts covering the narrow road that led to the vacation home where she was to join the other partners of Neufeldt in their annual cross-country skiing long weekend. Valentine's Day wasn't a holiday, of course, but the Monday of this coming weekend was an unofficial vacation day for many in the Province of Ontario. American companies would be celebrating Presidents' Day that day and many Canadian companies, whose business was tied to the US, gave their staff a day off. There was talk of making the day a vacation day, and calling it Family or Heritage Day, but so far nothing had come of that. For many of the other guests she would be meeting, this winter three-day weekend was an annual event, but it was the first time Pauline had been included. She was new to the firm, and this was her first winter with them.

Since leaving the highway and setting out along the narrow track leading to her boss's property, the short winter daylight had ended, and snow was falling steadily. When she'd driven out from the airport, the radio assured her the storm approaching from the west would track south of this northern area and she'd been heartily glad to hear that. Getting home on the Monday evening was a problem she didn't have to worry about. If she couldn't get back to Toronto and work, well then neither could her boss or most of the other partners who had also accepted this weekend retreat.

The trees on either side of the road loomed above the Jeep as it crunched over the thickening snow while the car's main beams lighted the tunnel that she appeared to be driving in. The sky and tall pines merged into one tube of darkness lit only by the car lights reflecting brightly along the snow. As the storm front was arriving, the snowflakes were growing bigger and falling heavier. The car's headlights were reflecting off them and what had been a long tunnel minutes ago, now seemed blocked by a white wall through which she could see nothing looking forward. All she'd heard about 'whiteouts' came back to her at once.

Mentally, she ran through all the safety aids the car rental salesman had shown her: snow shovel and mats; for if she got stuck, though the four-wheel drive would hopefully prevent that happening; blankets and candles to keep her warm until help arrived if all the above failed. A night in the wilderness with only a candle for heat wasn't something she relished. Adventures should end at teatime, Winnie-the-Pooh once said, and right now, she agreed with that amusing little bear who, if she remembered correctly, came from somewhere near here.

She could see nothing looking through the white wall of falling snow, even with the headlamps on low beam. The rear-view mirror also showed nothing but darkness behind. Surely the others she'd flown up with should be behind her. They were to be only a few minutes following her out of the airport. She regretted now staying in the office that extra time, finishing off what could have waited until next Tuesday. She really should have taken the midday flight the keener partygoers had taken. Her motivation for staying until the last flight of the day was partly a reluctance to leave work unfinished but, she had to admit, mainly a reluctance to take part in the Valentine's Day events her boss had planned. At fifty-three years old and steadfastly single throughout, she had little time for such nonsense.

Unfortunately, this desire to avoid awkward flirtatiousness meant she was arriving well after dark in a snowstorm. And if the others who'd stayed back until end of the workday weren't following her, as they'd said they would, she could expect no assistance if she ran off the road, which was beginning to seem ever more likely. She slowed the car to a crawl, judging her place on the lane by looking at the edge of the road out of the side window. It was dangerous but no more so than stopping would be. A car could run straight into the back of her if it was moving forward blindly as she was. That raised an equally horrible thought. As she drove on blindly, she could also run smack into the back of someone who was stopped up ahead.

Then, as quickly as it arrived, the snow squall stopped. Or maybe she'd just driven out of it. Either way, once again, she could see the road ahead. Sadly, she couldn't yet see any sign of lights to suggest she was getting closer to the lodge and the lake it was on. Gently pressing the accelerator, Pauline pushed the car forward. They'd told her the lodge was five miles from the main road. They'd actually said eight kilometers, but she'd have none of that metric nonsense which gave her no sense of distance. Unfortunately, she hadn't noted the mileage when she turned onto this sideroad and had no idea how far she had come or how much farther there was to go. She felt a great longing for her own warm apartment in Toronto, a good book, and a glass of sherry in front of her faux-log gas fire.

Moments later, as the vision of her apartment was growing warmer in her mind, the storm eased enough for her to see a glow of lights at the end of the tunnel of trees. A cottage or cottages lay a mile or so ahead and she had only to keep the car rolling steadily forward for another few minutes and she'd be safe. As she drew closer, she could see the lodge and the lake that lay frozen beyond it where matchstick figures were skiing or skating, black against the stark white snow that covered the frozen surface. All were palely lit with the lights from cottages and cars.

# 3

# THE OTHER GUESTS

RAUCOUS LAUGHTER from the lobby announced the arrival of the one of the youngest employees of Neufeldt, Tom Forrester and another young man, John Beresford, who worked in a competing firm. Their laughter was forced, as mirth often is when people are only a little acquainted. They entered the lounge area and greeted Jo and Saul.

"If there are any more guests on their way," John said, making his way to the window, "they'll be having a rotten time getting here."

"Mike went to phone the airport. He thought they could stop the other guests setting out," Saul said. "I hope they do catch them before they leave. We don't want anyone killed."

"Mike should have canceled the weekend when the weather forecast began to look iffy on Wednesday," Tom said, joining them at the window. "It was too risky, as we'd say in our report if we audited this in some other firm's business."

"The weather report wasn't so bad on Wednesday," Jo protested, "and you can't stop everything over a winter storm, not here in Canada. Otherwise, no one would ever do anything from November to April."

"I guess," Tom said. "Still, if someone's coming here along the sideroad right now, they must be wetting themselves." He gestured to the wall of white that was the window; nothing could be seen beyond the snow battering furiously against the glass.

"I'm sure they'll all have heard the weather on the flight up and they'll have taken rooms in a nearby motel," Saul said.

"Then it's going to be a small select party," Tom said. "Only the firm's most devoted staff, I reckon."

"Well, the ones who set out early anyhow," Jo replied sarcastically.

"Same thing," Tom replied, grinning. "At least, it is if we say it is. We're the auditors, after all."

The others were laughing when they saw Mike returning from his office with a worried expression.

"Some of them set out?" Saul asked.

"Only one," Mike replied. "Pauline left the airport before the news of the storm's change of direction was announced. Or at least that's what Ben said. She wanted her own car, and the rental place served her first. The others said they'd catch her up but when they were signing the papers, the radio said not to head out, so they didn't."

"Why didn't she wait for the others?" Tom said. "Surely traveling in a convoy would have made sense."

"Pauline likes to be her own woman," Jo said. Her tone didn't make it sound complimentary.

"She would be expecting them to catch her up, I expect," Mike said. "I'm afraid I was a bit short with Ben. Leaving anyone, let alone a single woman, to drive in this weather on their own is bad."

"Pauline's a good driver," Jo said. "She says so."

"Even good drivers crash when they can't see the road," Mike said, angrily. "If anything happens to her..." He let the sentence die away. "What would I tell her folks back in England?"

"The truth," Jo replied, as no one else seemed to be about to jump in. "She was caught out on the road in a bad winter storm. It's nobody's fault. Not yours, not ours. Pauline is devout, though she doesn't make a thing of it, I'm happy to say. She'll understand it was her time."

Mike's expression grew thunderous at this callous remark, but he was diverted by the entrance of an elderly man. The oldest of the firm's employees, Bryan O' Connell.

"What's up, Mike?" Bryan asked, seeing the tension in their postures and feeling it in the air.

"Pauline Riddell is somewhere on the road heading here," Mike said. "She's on her own and doesn't know the road."

"Have I met her?" Bryan asked.

Mike shook his head. "She's fairly new and you're never around to be introduced."

"Maybe she'll pull off at a farm or something if it's too dangerous to go on," Bryan said.

"There aren't farms here, Bryan," Mike said.

"Well, a cottage or something. It's too soon to worry. The storm has only just started, she may be just along the road and will be here at any moment."

"Bryan's right," Saul said. "There's no reason to suppose any harm will come to her."

"Should we take a car back down the road to look?" John asked uncertainly. He was an outsider and the youngest there and wasn't sure how his suggesting such a risky undertaking would be viewed.

Mike shook his head. "It's a good thought, John, but we could end up with more people stranded. We'll wait. This may pass over and if she isn't here when it ends, we'll head out then. Let's continue with our evening. Like Bryan said, it's too soon to worry."

Despite Mike's cheerful tone, it was a subdued group that headed off to the games room to pour drinks and arrange teams for pool and darts, the two principal games on offer.

# 4

# ARRIVAL

Pauline, with a fervent prayer of thanks, pulled into the driveway of the lodge and parked alongside the cars of the other guests. The door of the lodge opened, sending a bright beam of light out into the darkness, and a middle-aged man, warmly dressed against the driving snow gathering on his coat, strode out toward her car. Pauline pulled up the hood of her own coat and climbed stiffly out of the Jeep, surprised to find how difficult that felt. Despite the car's heater, her thick winter coat, and tweed business jacket and skirt, she still felt chilled to the marrow. Stress was bad for the muscles, she thought, as she was hailed by the approaching man.

"Miss Riddell?" he asked.

"Present," Pauline said, remembering schooldays.

"I'm Laurent Pomerleau," the man said. "My wife, Catrina, and I are helping out here this weekend. Catrina's doing the cooking, I'm doing the *butling*, or whatever it is butlers do. Where are your bags?"

Pauline was about to protest she could carry her own

bags but realized this was idiotic. Pomerleau was hired to help.

"In the trunk," Pauline said, opening the rear door.

"We were getting worried," Pomerleau said. "The weather's closing in. It's not good to be caught on the road out here when there's a storm rolling through."

Pauline grinned. "I got a hint of that only a mile or so back there," she said, pointing along the way she'd come. "The snow's not so heavy here." She followed him into the house. "Am I last to arrive?" Pauline continued, as they crossed the cavernous lobby heading for the broad open staircase that led up the second floor.

"We think so. More were coming but they're taking a room in North Bay tonight," he replied. "They'll drive up tomorrow if the roads are okay. Hopefully, no one is still *on* the road because they're now saying the storm is tracking further north than expected and we'll get more snow than they originally thought."

Pauline nodded. "If I'd heard that at the airport," she said, "I'd have waited until morning before setting out."

He led her into a spacious bedroom with a bed big enough for a party to take place in and left her to unwind and unpack, saying, "Supper is at seven; you haven't long to get ready."

After a shower and change of clothes, Pauline made her way downstairs to where she could hear voices, laughter, and the clink of glasses. She hoped they had sherry, and lots of it.

"Pauline," her boss, Mike Armitage called, as Pauline made her way down the wide stairs to the ground floor. It was like being on one of those Hollywood film sets where the star descended to a waiting, adoring public. Sadly,

Pauline thought, she wasn't a glamorous star, and the waiting public weren't adoring.

Mike was the firm's senior partner and had been made CEO of Neufeldt and Partners when it was taken over by the global corporation Ed Seaforth had been hoping to sell his company to when Pauline worked there. As she made her way toward the party, he said, "Let me introduce you to everyone."

The lodge had belonged to Mike's family for a long time and had grown over the years as his father, and now he, had become wealthy. Today, it was the size of a small wilderness resort. And like a resort, it had its own shoreline on the lake and a surrounding forest for guests to explore on foot in warmer weather or quad bike in all seasons. Mike had assured Pauline she'd love driving the snow-covered logging trails on a snowmobile or quad bike. Pauline, however, had reserved judgment on the promised treat, only smiling in what she hoped was a sufficiently non-committal way.

As Pauline joined them, she said, "I think I know almost everyone."

She smiled and nodded to Gilles Ouimet who was grinning at her. He'd left Seaforth and joined Neufeldt only weeks before she had. Ed Seaforth, it turned out, had been right. Once, the global company had swallowed Neufeldt, Seaforth's clients began abandoning the company almost daily, until there wasn't enough business left for its staff.

Pauline had been sorry to leave Seaforth. She really had hoped Jerry Seaforth, Ed's daughter, could find a way to keep the company going. She couldn't and Ed's funeral, which Pauline had attended, had come only two months after the cruel affair of Ed's youngest daughter's murder. Though it shouldn't have done, the funeral brought an end to her involvement with the Seaforth family and that was soon followed by her leaving their firm.

"Well, of course you know our people, but do you know John Beresford?" Mike said, turning to a young man standing beside him.

"I don't," Pauline said, shaking his hand.

"I'm hoping to lure John into joining us," Mike explained. "He's something of a rising star in the local profession and, I understand, politics."

John laughed. "Mike is flattering me," he said. "I've joined the local Liberal Party in my constituency. No more than that. And as for the profession, I'm on the committee of our local branch of the Chartered Professional Accountants of Canada."

John was mid-to-late twenties, still boyish looking, with an engaging smile hovering around his eyes as though he viewed life as a happy event. That appearance was aided by a shock of unruly chestnut hair that made Pauline want to comb it; she suspected every woman who met him would feel much the same.

"Still, those are statements of ambition and intent," Pauline said. "Mike is right to be interested."

"Do you know Bryan O' Connell?" Mike said, gesturing to an older man, white-haired, stooped, and skinny. He looked like he needed more than one good meal. "He's been a fixture at Neufeldt since I don't know when. Long before my time, anyhow."

"I don't think we've met," Pauline said, smiling, though she was puzzled. How was it she'd been in the office every day for nearly six months now and never met this relic? She offered her hand, which he took.

"How do you do," Pauline said, shaking his hand. It was

an elderly handshake without vigor or warmth. "I can't understand how we haven't met."

"I don't get into the office much these days," Bryan said quietly. "My clients are old like me, and we tend to meet at their offices. I gave up mine long ago."

"I see," Pauline said, though she didn't.

"You must have been caught in that squall we watched from the window," Gilles said. "It looked pretty nasty." Gilles was just Gilles, Pauline thought. A bear of a man. The only man she'd ever met who matched the description *barrel-chested*. You could imagine him both lifting barrels and drinking them dry.

"It was," Pauline replied. "I hope there's no one on the road behind me."

Mike shook his head. "No one," he said. "They've all called in now, and everyone is accounted for. Some didn't travel at all, and some are staying overnight in North Bay. If it's safe, they plan to drive up in the morning."

"They're wise," Pauline said. "I only had fifteen minutes of that whiteout and I was wishing I'd stayed home too."

"The good news," John Beresford said, "is the storm will pass over tonight and we'll have great snow for skiing tomorrow."

Mike laughed. "More like snowshoeing," he said. "There's no way we can get trails groomed if it's as bad as they say it will be." As he spoke, he turned to another young man, saying, "And here's our newest recruit, Tom."

Pauline turned to see a man in his twenties standing quietly behind John. He was medium height, medium build, and medium coloring. He just looked average, everything an accountant was supposed to be, Pauline thought with a smile. He may be clever – he wouldn't have been hired if he wasn't – but not the standout kind of personality Beresford seemed.

They shook hands and Pauline asked where he'd been before joining the firm.

"Uni," Tom said. "I'm straight from school to Neufeldt and Partners. I feel like I won the lottery."

"And so you did," Mike said, grinning, "but don't worry, we'll work you so hard you'll wish you'd gone to some lesser company."

As the conversations her arrival had interrupted began again, Pauline noticed that while the two young men appeared to have formed an alliance of the young, there was a constraint between Tom and John that showed in the way they talked too loudly and the way they competed for attention. She smiled inwardly to herself; two young males eager to demonstrate their fitness to the Alpha in the room by doing down the other. An ancient instinct but one that drove almost everything that happened in the world, for good or bad.

Pauline turned away from gazing at the two young men and saw another guest joining them. He came from a corridor at the farthest side of this main lobby, and she recognized him at once, though it had been more than five years since they'd last met.

"Do you know Arnie Hamilton?" Mike asked Pauline. "He used to work at Seaforth but that may have been before your time."

Pauline smiled, though she felt it wouldn't convey much warmth. "I worked with Arnie on my very first Seaforth audit," she said. As they shook hands, she asked, "Are you with Neufeldt now?"

"No," he replied. "Mike and I know each other from

being in the same business for years. I'm the competition right now."

"But we're working on changing that," Mike said, grinning.

"Well, it's nice to see you again, Arnie," Pauline said, before her attention was caught by two more people approaching.

"And here are the last of our earlier arrivals," Mike said, gesturing toward the wide staircase that led from the ground to the upper floor, "both of whom I'm sure you know. Saul and Jo," he paused, before adding, "sounds a bit like one of those pop groups, doesn't it?"

"I know Jo and Saul," Pauline said, nodding welcome to them as they approached. She didn't like either of them. They were both aggressive and opinionated, and, Pauline felt, in Jo's case anyhow, appeared threatened by Pauline's arrival in the company. In Pauline's opinion, Jo had been riding the tide of female empowerment to the upper echelons of Neufeldt and she saw Pauline as diluting that advantage.

5

## OMINOUS SIGNS

"It's started again," Gilles said, pointing out of the full wall-to-ceiling window, where snowflakes swirled in the light shining out from the room.

"You have a backup generator if we lose power, don't you Mike?" O'Connell asked, clearly nervous at the prospect of a night without power.

"We do, Bryan, and we've a stack of wood large enough to get us through until the spring thaw, don't you worry."

"At my age, I worry about a lot," O'Connell replied morosely.

"It would be like the pioneers lived if the lights went out," Tom said, grinning. He clearly thought this something worth looking forward to.

A discussion began as to what pioneering this far north would have really been like and Pauline had the opportunity to get the measure of her fellow guests. For herself, she couldn't help remembering she'd once read that one of the young boy officers on the Franklin Expedition in 1845 had written home to his family saying that though they were supposed to be out of the Northwest

Passage before winter set in, he hoped they would experience at least one winter in the Arctic. He'd gotten his wish; he and all the others had spent every winter since then in the Arctic.

She gave herself a mental shake. That couldn't happen today. There were many ways they could escape from the lodge if the power failed and the log fires couldn't keep the building temperature up. They were quite safe. If the storm brought down the power lines, they'd have an adventure. Nothing more than an adventure.

"What say you, Pauline?" Mike asked, breaking into her reverie.

"I'm sorry. I missed what you were saying."

"We were talking about skiing on the lake at first light," Tom said. "The snow will be untouched then, not cut up as it will be when the snowmobilers get up and out. And there'll be no nasty surprises under the drifts as there are sometimes in the forest where a fallen branch can trip unwary skiers."

Pauline smiled. "I'll make my decision in the morning, when I know for sure the storm has passed through and I've seen what it has dumped on us."

Mike laughed. "A wise answer," he said, "but I'm sure it will be fine. We've never been snowed in here in all the years we've been coming, and this was my family's place before mine." He paused, before adding, "Now, let me close the blinds and get back to celebrating St. Valentine." He took a small remote device from a holster on the wall, pressed a button and window coverings rolled smoothly across the glass, cutting out the brightly lit snow and dark shadows.

"I say we celebrate with a game of pool," Beresford said. "You have a great games room, Mike."

"It has everything a man needs," Mike replied, grinning. "Pool, TV, darts, poker, and a bar."

The party moved to the games room, pool teams were formed and playing times established. Those who were waiting for their turn at pool, began a darts league. Beers were opened, and the party, which had been restrained before, began growing loud with challenge and counterchallenge, enthusiastic support and loud derision, and boisterous laughter. Pauline, who'd found sherry in the lounge's drinks cabinet, sipped at her glass and watched quietly as the games progressed.

None of the players seemed markedly better than the others, though the younger men and Arnie made extravagant boasts about their achievements; their bragging, however, remained amicable for which she was thankful. When it was her go, Pauline took her turn at pool, at which she was poor, and darts, which she'd played since a child and was consequently better at than most of the others.

"You've practiced, Pauline," John said, grinning. "That's not fair."

"I'm sure you've all played before too," Pauline responded, "so it's equal."

"You've won two games in a row," Arnie said. "That's why young Mr. Beresford is crying foul."

"And lost at pool by a landslide," Pauline said. "I notice no one complained about that!"

John laughed. "You're right," he said. "We only complain when we lose. Isn't that the way of everybody?"

"Perhaps," Pauline said. It seemed the best way to end the discussion.

"You used to work at Seaforth, I hear," John said, not taking the hint.

"I did."

"You were lucky to get out in time," John said.

Their conversation was briefly interrupted by Saul shouting, "Hey, you two. You're up next for pool. Don't hold up the table, it's getting exciting."

"You mean you're leading the pack on wins," Tom mocked him.

"That's right. I'll be crowned champion soon if those two stop wasting our precious time and get over here and play."

Pauline and John grinned at each other and did as they were told. "You can start," Pauline said. "It won't make any difference to the result."

John took his shot and, with the game underway, they returned to their conversation.

"You're right about me being lucky to get out of Seaforth before the end," Pauline said. "It's sad to see it sinking. I really liked Ed Seaforth."

"Before my time," John said, preparing to take his shot. "I only know because when we were doing the rounds of prospective employers that last year of university, the end of Seaforth was what everyone was talking about and we were advised us not to go there."

"I'm surprised they were hiring," Pauline said, watching as John pocketed another ball.

"The rumor was it was to replace the people leaving." John straightened up when his shot hit the pocket but rebounded. He stepped aside to let Pauline have one of her few opportunities.

"Did anyone go for an interview with them?" Pauline asked, when once again, she failed to hit the ball cleanly, and it missed the pocket.

"I don't think so," John said, ending the game with a clean shot.

"You still won't catch me," Saul shouted to John, as he

marked up the scores. "The crown is mine." He laughed as his boast was greeted by a chorus of derision.

"You're happy where you are though?" Pauline asked John. "Or is that why you're considering a move to Neufeldt?"

"I'm happy enough but when someone wants you, it's hard to resist," John said. "We all love to be wanted, don't we?"

Pauline laughed. "We do," she said. "Well, it's my turn at the dart board again so I wish you luck for a large inducement to join us at Neufeldt."

After her game, Pauline took the opportunity to slip away and refill her glass. She was alone at the drinks' cabinet and the noise from the games room was subdued by distance and the door. The Pomerleaus seemed to be arguing so, with her glass refilled, Pauline sauntered casually across the lobby to hear what was being said. She took up a station near the lodge's front door that gave her a view down the road and was close enough to hear the Pomerleaus' conversation.

"This is a storm that could isolate us for days. I want to be home not stuck here. What's so hard to understand about that?" Pauline heard Catrina say.

"The storm is already on us," Laurent replied. "We'd be crazy to drive out in this."

"If we'd left when I said—"

"But we couldn't, could we," Laurent interjected.

"I can't keep out of his way forever," Catrina said. "Not if we're all stuck here."

"I'm here too, remember."

"You assume I'm afraid what he might do?" Catrina said scornfully.

Before Laurent could respond, with Pauline straining

every nerve to hear his reply, the games room door opened and Gilles bellowed, “Pauline, you’re up for pool.”

Fuming, Pauline crossed the lobby and re-entered the games room. Of all the times to interrupt, she thought. Her frustration didn’t help her play and the game was soon over.

Once again, Pauline quietly slipped out of the room, but the Pomerleau conversation had moved on and it was all about getting ready for serving the evening meal. She re-joined the party, observing and listening to their conversations instead. It had often occurred to her that, if she hadn’t fallen into investigating by chance, she would have found her way into some kind of occupation where watching her fellow man would have happened naturally.

As the evening wore on, however, Pauline, found herself longing for the quiet of her room. In small numbers or small doses, she could manage people, but when the noise and bustle grew too intense, it left her drained, weary even. By late evening, when even the most lively of her fellow guests were wilting, the party broke into smaller groups discussing sport, the weather, and their plans for the morning. These safe topics lasted until one by one, the guests drifted off to their rooms, citing the early start as their reason for leaving. When it seemed her leaving wouldn’t be commented on, Pauline wished the remainder good night and went off to her room to read.

# 6

# PAULINE WARNS MIKE

THE WIND that had moaned around the lodge, waking her repeatedly through the night, had died by morning and Pauline looked out of her bedroom window on a freshly fallen shroud of snow, shining in the just rising sunlight. Overhead the sky was the palest of blues; washed out, she thought it. There was no escaping her fate. Despite her misgivings, she couldn't fault the snow or the weather and would have to ski with the others. Every winter in Canada increased her confidence on skis and skates but she still felt one day she'd injure herself. She was an old dog learning new tricks and felt that keenly.

The breakfast room was filled with her colleagues when she arrived. Coffee and a muffin were the meal of choice as they urged each other to be outside in minutes. Pauline drank her tea, especially made for her in a real teapot by the attentive Catrina and joined the others in the mud room where the skis were kept.

"Follow me," Mike said. "We'll go down the road to the lakeshore in a gentle slalom and ski straight onto the lake."

He stepped outside and began clipping his skis onto his shoes. The others followed.

As she fastened her skis to her shoes, Pauline noted that Arnie Hamilton was his usual saturnine self and looking strangely rebellious, though what kind of rebellion he could act out here, Pauline couldn't imagine.

Seeing the group ready to go, Mike turned and began skating his skis, accelerating out of the parking lot and onto the gentle slope down to the road. Pauline waited to let the others pass. They would almost certainly be quicker than she was, and she didn't want them overtaking her on the narrow road she could see at the bottom of the slope. She was about to move when she heard a muttered growl behind her. She turned to see Arnie surveying the bushes along the side of the parking lot where an opening suggested a path may lead down to the lake. He seemed about to dive into the bushes.

Alarmed, Pauline said, "These are cross-country skis, Arnie, not Alpine ones."

He snorted derisively. "Scandinavians go down steeper hills than this with these kinds of skis," he said, shaking his right ski in the air, before pausing as though unsure how to go on. "By the way," he finally added, "in case you're wondering, I don't have a grudge against you because you alerted Ed Seaforth to what I was doing, all those years ago."

"I'm happy to hear it," Pauline said. "It would make for an awkward weekend if you did."

He grinned. "You played fair," he said. "You argued against what I was doing and told me upfront your concerns. You had to tell Ed really."

"If things had gone differently," Pauline reminded him, "it would have destroyed Seaforth and Partners."

He laughed again. "It wouldn't have gone differently," he

said. "Those guys were criminals and I had them squirming. They had no come back against any of us, except me, and their kind don't frighten me."

"Well, they should," Pauline said. "There are usually gangsters behind swindles of that kind."

"This is why I now have my own company and I'm always in demand, while you still work for a firm of accountants," Arnie said. "You and your colleagues expose honest one-off mistakes made by some poor sucker who tries to cover it up or often just honest misunderstandings of the rules that benefit no-one. I go after the real criminals. Maybe that's why I'm invited here."

Pauline frowned. "I hope not," she said, but he wasn't listening. He was already heading into the trees at the side of the parking lot.

"What are you doing?" she called to his retreating back. "You'll break your neck."

"Live fast, die young and have a good-looking corpse; that's my motto. That road is too tame for me," he said, with a manic laugh. A firm push on his poles and he disappeared into the thicket of snow-covered branches. He was soon lost to sight.

As she made her own way sedately down the driveway to the road, she could hear his progress, and his coarse expletives when he met something hazardous. His progress appeared slower even than her own and she paused to admire the view. If something went wrong, she felt she should have an idea how far along the trail his body lay.

The road was a snow-white lane leading down the lake. Mike and her fellow guests were gathered on the smooth white carpet that stretched clear and level all the way to the cottages on the other side. From their chimneys, smoke rose lazily in the still air. It was a beautiful morning, crisply cold, but, Pauline wondered, was it just the eye of the storm? If so, she didn't want to be caught too far out on the lake and faraway from the lodge. When she was sure Arnie must be down by now, she gave a gentle push on her poles and slid her skis around until they were pointing downhill. Her exhilaration mounted as her speed increased.

As Pauline slid gracefully to a stop among the group, Mike asked, "Where's Arnie?"

"He said the road was too tame..." Pauline began but before she could say more Arnie burst out of a thicket and landed on the frozen lake with a jarring thump, laughing wildly. He began skating his skis, powerfully driving through the soft snow and farther out onto the lake, heading exactly the opposite way the group was going. That was Arnie, Pauline thought grimly.

"That's my boy," Mike said, grinning, with a proud parent expression on his face.

Pauline's heart sank. Mike wasn't married and had no kids so she feared he really might have come to regard Arnie as the son he never had. As Pauline was planning to warn Mike against hiring Arnie, Mike's obvious admiration complicated the already difficult advice she wanted to give.

"Who can catch Arnie?" Mike shouted, turning and setting off in pursuit. The younger men, Tom, John and even Saul were soon close behind him, leaving Pauline, Gilles, Bryan and Jo staring after them wistfully.

"Boys and their toys," Jo said, disdainfully.

Pauline smiled. Female solidarity should have her agreeing with Jo, but she just couldn't.

"If we could really ski," Pauline said, "we could chase them too."

"I can ski," Jo snapped.

"Then don't let me keep you," Pauline said. "How about you, Gilles, Bryan?"

Gilles smiled and shook his head.

Bryan laughed. "Strictly a city park skier me," he said. "We should go the other way to show we don't hold with such childish nonsense."

"I agree," Pauline said. "Without women to show off to, they'll soon come back." As the men's voices echoing across the lake were growing more distant, Pauline said this with more hope than conviction.

They continued along the lake in a single file, Bryan cutting a trail and the other three following until Jo, with an exaggerated sigh, overtook him and they followed her.

When she'd gotten far enough ahead for them to be private, Pauline said quietly to Bryan and Gilles, "Girls and their toys."

Bryan laughed. "Competitive people never like it when others are better than them in anything; I've noticed that down the years."

"And they'll say or do anything to prevent anyone else exceling," Pauline said.

Bryan nodded. "I used to tell my kids there were only two ways of being the best. Either practice so hard you *were* the best or make everyone else worse than you. I've found the second way is the most usual, most common, in everyday life."

Pauline laughed. His comment, though it agreed with her own assessment of how the world worked, suggested a bitterness that was more than just the ennui the old have for a world they're no longer part of.

"You're too censorious," Pauline said. "There's always a bit of both." She decided, when she had the opportunity, she'd learn more about the mysterious Bryan who was a colleague but one she'd never seen until this weekend.

Gilles, who'd been bringing up the rear of their small party, said, "Seems like you were right, as usual, Pauline."

A growing noise of revelry, and that usual loud male banter, approaching quickly behind her, made Pauline glance over her shoulder. Her prediction had indeed been correct. Without Jo to show off to, the men had soon lost interest in their race down the lake and were now racing up the lake.

"Come on Pauline," Arnie, who was still leading the pack, shouted. "Leave the old guys and get your heart pumping with us."

Pauline waved him goodbye as he sped on past her, then Bryan, and was soon chasing down Jo. At least Jo will be pleased, Pauline thought smiling. And they would make a well-matched couple, she thought somewhat unkindly.

"I'll join you three," Mike said as he slowed to a halt beside Pauline. "That way it won't look like I couldn't keep up." He grinned, his white teeth gleaming in the brilliant sunshine.

"I won't tell," Pauline said, maintaining the humorous thrust to the conversation though her mind was focused on the thin, gray clouds approaching from the southwest, which she could see over Mike's shoulder.

"I know I can trust you to keep a secret, Pauline," Mike began. Then, noticing her gaze was behind him, he looked over his shoulder. "Where did they come from," he said, frowning. "It was clear skies all the way when we were going down the lake."

Pauline nodded. "They're coming quickly," she said. "Even as I've been watching they've covered much of the sky. We need to head back."

Mike nodded. "Hallo-o-o," he shouted, hoping to get the attention of Arnie and Jo who were now racing out farther onto the lake. Arnie's powerful, aggressive style quickly closing the gap on Jo's elegant, yet swift moving form. Like a lion after a gazelle, Pauline thought with a shiver.

Jo heard Mike's call, echoing across the lake, and paused, allowing her skis to skim over the surface and lose momentum. When Mike pointed at the fast-moving storm, Jo turned, signaled to Arnie and the two quickly changed direction and began racing back to the group.

Pauline and the others also turned and began heading back to the road and safety. Their slow progress on the way out had allowed them plenty of energy to pick up their pace on the return; nevertheless, Jo and Arnie were at the road ahead of them. A thin rain that froze the moment it landed on anything was falling as they struggled up the road to the lodge and a sharp wind blew icy rain into their faces.

By the time she'd reached the lodge, Pauline was wishing she'd never agreed to come on this 'fun weekend'. The physical discomfort of being drenched in icy rain was only matched by the mental discomfort she felt knowing she had to alert Mike to the danger he was in by enticing Arnie into the firm. How was she going to get time alone with Mike to tell him what she knew?

Later that afternoon, after the group had exhausted the topic of the storm, which the radio described as a Colorado Clipper, and all the usual board games that a northern cottage contained, Pauline simply asked to speak to Mike privately.

As he led the way into his office at the rear of the house, Mike asked, "What's so important, Pauline? You can't leave if that's what you're thinking. The roads will be ice-covered until tomorrow at the earliest."

As Pauline had heard the same gloomy weather updates he'd listened to, she wondered how he could be so flippant. The weather service was advising no travel at all in the next twenty-four hours throughout all this region and even farther south toward the Great Lakes.

As Mike took a seat by the window and suggested she take the one opposite, Pauline began, "I have the sense you're considering Arnie for a position in the firm." She sat and swiveled the chair, so she wasn't looking at the sheet of ice the window had become. It made her shiver just to see it.

"We need his kind of drive for some of the cases we've been getting lately," Mike said.

Pauline frowned. She knew what he was referring to but couldn't agree with the solution.

"I worked with Arnie on my very first audit when I joined Seaforth," she said at last. "I want to tell you about it. I know it's six years ago and Arnie may have toned down his methods a little, but it almost destroyed Seaforth and could do the same for Neufeldt."

"Seaforth destroyed themselves in the end," Mike said, "so I'm not sure the view from Seaforth is necessarily a good guide."

"The two things aren't related," Pauline replied, growing more unhappy at his flippancy with every minute.

"The audit you're referring to, however, was incredibly successful," Mike said. "Three criminals went to jail."

Pauline nodded. "And they deserved to," she said. "What they were doing seemed harmless enough to them perhaps, but the money was being funneled to truly criminal people," she paused, then added, "but Arnie did things that were practically criminal himself and earned the wrath of the police and judge at the trial. It blackened Seaforth's name for months, maybe years, after."

"What you say may be true, Pauline," Mike replied, "but since then Arnie has been solidly employed by people, including government agencies, to get to the bottom of some pretty nasty swindles. People may not entirely approve of his methods, but they do appreciate the results. I'd like some of that business coming our way."

"His methods...," Pauline began, but stopped when her boss held up his hand.

"His methods are extreme, but they are always legal and in today's business world, we need results not high principles. The time for high-minded Victorian virtues is well and truly over. Arnie has shown us all the way and I mean to have him on our team," Mike said, bluntly.

"Well, I felt you should know how much damage his methods can cause but I see you've considered that and feel they're no longer a threat," Pauline said. "Maybe you're right. However, if he does come on board, I hope there will never be an occasion for me to work with him. I couldn't reconcile that with my conscience. I found the experience last time enough for one lifetime."

Mike laughed. "I'll see he doesn't work with you, if he joins us," he said. He hesitated and then added, "You really don't like him, do you?'

"Neither as a person nor as a professional," Pauline said. "Now, I should let you get back to your other guests. I've monopolized your time more than I should." She rose and left him grinning after her in what she thought was a satirical way. *He thinks I'm an old cat for this warning*. She left, closing the office door behind her. She shook her head to clear it. She could only hope Arnie was doing too well on his own to join Neufeldt and her worst fears wouldn't happen.

She rejoined the others in the lobby where Arnie and Jo

were dancing to music that was deafening. It was so loud it took Pauline some moments to realize it was a song she liked, *Walk of Life* by Dire Straits, a group from her old home of Newcastle-upon-Tyne. For a moment, Pauline stood in nostalgic memories and then slipped by the dancers into the lounge, with its picture windows overlooking the lake. There, the more restrained guests were drinking and talking about the weather, which they could see wasn't improving.

"I'm not skiing in that ice tomorrow," Bryan was saying as Pauline entered the room. "At my age, you get nervous about falls."

"I don't think we'll even get out of the door, if it doesn't stop soon," Tom said. "The ice on those trees must be inches thick even now." As he spoke, a branch from a tree across the parking lot fell, taking the branches below with it, clearing almost the whole side of the tree. "See what I mean?" he said.

Pauline joined them at the window. She could almost feel their nervous excitement. The force of the storm was exhilarating but the thought the house could lose all power and heat if a tree brought down electrical lines somewhere nearby tempered her own enthusiasm.

"So much for weather forecasters," Pauline said. "This, and the snowstorm before it, was supposed to track farther south and miss us completely."

"Maybe we can sue," Saul said, grinning.

"That's why they call it forecasting," Bryan said. "So, you can't sue them."

"Mike says there's enough wood to keep the fires going, if all else fails," John said. "I hope he's right. We'll each need a fire in our bedrooms tonight if the power goes out before we retire."

"That's true," Bryan said, frowning. "In fact, I'm going to

get Pomerleau to light one in my room now. Better safe than sorry." He marched away toward the kitchen where the Pomerleaus could be heard working.

"What an old woman," Tom said.

"Speaking as an older woman," Pauline said, smiling, "I'd like to point out it is a man and not a woman who is the first to go looking to his personal and private comforts."

Tom grinned. "True," he said, "but it doesn't change my mind about old Bryan."

"Can someone tell me about Bryan?" Pauline asked. "I hadn't heard of him until yesterday and apparently he works in the firm and has done so for years."

Saul said, "He's still in the firm because it was agreed that way. He was the next in line to be the head of the company, but, when the time came, the selection committee chose Mike. Bryan was given lifetime employment in exchange. He's making them pay by continuing to draw a salary instead of a pension and he appears once in a blue moon to remind the partners of their treachery. Basically, that's it. He's bitter and resentful and takes it out on the firm in every way he can, but in a civilized manner, of course."

"I see," Pauline said. "How awful. He must feel like a ghost or a zombie, wandering the building without a place to rest."

"A vengeful one," Saul said, seriously. "Be careful around Bryan. He's a nice man, a good man, but he was wronged and that's a dangerous mix. People have written stories about that since time began and they always end badly for someone."

"I will," Pauline said. "However, I'm too new to incur his wrath, so I think I'm safe."

"But they hired you when they already had him there doing nothing," Saul said. "You may not be to blame for that decision, but you shouldn't assume you're safe from the feelings such a rejection may have created. You too, Gilles. You were also hired when Bryan was in limbo."

"Oh, great," Gilles, said, grinning. "I'll wedge my bedroom door shut when I go up."

Pauline smiled. "I too shall be on my guard." As she finished speaking, the windows shook with a fearsome blast and ice slid down the panes. "I think," Pauline added, "I'll follow Bryan's lead and have a fire lit in my room tonight as well." She paused, then added, fixing Tom with a fierce stare, "After all, I am an older woman."

Tom laughed, a little nervously, Pauline thought with satisfaction, as she made her way to where she could hear Laurent Pomerleau and Bryan talking.

"Laurent," Pauline said, when the two stopped to find what she wanted, 'I've come to add my request to Bryan's. I'd like a fire lit in my room too. I don't have confidence the power will survive the night and I'd like something to keep me warm."

"There," Bryan said to Laurent, triumphantly. "I told you everyone would want the same soon. It looks bad out there and power lines are flimsy things to hang your life on."

"Even if the power went out," Laurent said, exasperated. "There's enough insulation in the logs to maintain the heat until it comes back. Trust me, on this."

Bryan shook his head. "At my time of life, the circulation isn't what it was. My toes and fingers are cold even now. Here," he added, holding out his hand, "feel."

"Okay, okay," Laurent said, avoiding Bryan's outstretched hand. "Fires all round." He turned and headed back to the kitchen.

"I hope he's gone for wood and firelighters," Pauline said, puzzled at his abrupt departure. She was reassured a few moments later when Laurent returned with a hamper of logs and papers.

"By the time you go to bed," Laurent said, "the fires will be going good." He set off upstairs muttering darkly.

"Actually, I'm thinking of going to bed soon," Pauline said, as she and Bryan returned slowly to the main area. Their two fellow guests, Jo and Arnie, were still dancing to deafening rock music that Pauline again vaguely recognized. She thought it was Canada's own group of theatrical rockers, Rush, but she wasn't a fan, and it could have been any one of the heavy metal groups currently in fashion.

While they'd been talking to Laurent, the debate in the games room on sports issues had grown lively with the downing of more beers and shots. The tone was turning into what Pauline knew men loved but she didn't – locker room trash talk. It made her even more determined to leave the party early.

Her excuses were met by requests for her to stay, 'it was too early for bed' and 'there was much to be discussed that she could contribute to'. This last was clearly not true for Pauline disliked all professional sports and never watched them.

Pauline shook her head. "Sorry," she said, "the cold this morning and the noise from the music in the next room have brought on a headache. I'll just lie down for a while until it passes."

In her room, the fire in the woodburning stove was burning nicely. Pauline pulled up a chair, closed the curtains – shutting out the storm still raging – opened her book, and enjoyed a quiet afternoon at home, almost.

# 7

# A MURDER HAPPENS

AT SEVEN, she heard people gathering for the evening meal and went down to join them. To her amazement, Jo and Arnie were just wrapping up their dance session. One quick look at their eyes when they entered the dining area showed her how they'd managed the marathon. One of them had brought some powerful stimulants. She was liking this weekend even less now that she was learning more about her fellow guests.

After supper, they gathered in front of the log fire in the reception area of the lodge and the talk was animated. The storm, and when it might end, was the principal discussion, particularly as the TV news was showing the damage it was wreaking on roads, homes, and power supplies farther south. Pauline made a note to take extra wood upstairs when she returned to her room.

The men drifted away to the games room and Jo followed with Arnie trailing along behind, though Pauline sensed both wanted to be somewhere more private. There was a twitchiness about them that wasn't all drug induced. When the party finally said they were too bushed to play pool, Pauline took the opportunity to find Laurent and pick up more wood.

She deposited her extra logs on the brick hearth the stove stood on, returning to her easy chair and book with a feeling of great contentment. It was almost midnight before the music and voices she could hear from below died away and the house was quiet. She closed her book, rose, and made her way to the room's en-suite bathroom. Away from the fire, the room felt cold. She didn't spend long preparing for bed. Once in bed, she was soon asleep.

Around two, she woke. Her digital bedside clock, whose pale green light had been shining when she'd switched out the bedside light, was dark. A power cut. Pauline slipped out of bed. The room was even colder, though the fire still glowed in the grate. She put another log on it and opened the curtains. Her room looked out to the lake where everything was in darkness. Earlier, there'd been lights from cottages around the shoreline, now there were none. It wasn't just the lodge that had lost power. The whole district seemed down. Pauline remembered Mike saying there was a generator and hoped Laurent Pomerleau would have the power back on to the lodge before she had to get out of bed in the morning.

When she woke next, Pomerleau clearly had gotten the generator running or the power was back on because she could hear the Pomerleaus bustling around downstairs. Her bedside alarm clock's digital screen, however, was still blank. It was seven am, according to her watch.

Pauline lay quietly wondering how she was going to get through the rest of this weekend. Without the cross-country skiing or snowmobiling, the other fun diversion they'd been promised, they would want to talk about business, which she had no taste for, playing pool, which she had even less taste for, watching TV, which she refused to do, or the inevitable board games every northern home had in abundance. On balance, she thought a day of playing Trivial Pursuit and Monopoly the better path forward.

As dawn lightened the curtains, the storm had clearly abated. Pauline rose from the bed and crossed to the window. Outside, daylight was only just creeping across the forest and lake, which lay under its smooth, now icy, cover of snow. No one was out on the frozen lake. Perhaps it was too early or perhaps the thick coating of ice on everything made it too hazardous. She let go of the curtains and returned to bed.

She'd only been back under the covers a moment when she realized the voices she could hear were getting closer. She slipped out of bed and put on her robe to find out what was happening. Even as she was fastening her robe, there was a knock on her door and she heard Mike say, "Pauline would you come and look at this, please?"

She followed him along the corridor to an open door in what she knew was Arnie's room. Mike signaled her to follow him inside, which she did. She had only to step through the door to see why Mike had brought her here.

Arnie's body lay on its side, as if sleeping, but the gaping hole where his right temple should have been, told a different story. Arnie was dead. A ski pole, its spike covered in blood, lay beside the body.

## 8

## PAULINE AT THE CRIME SCENE

"PAULINE," Mike said, his voice quiet and deadly serious, "I asked you here to see this for two reasons. One, you have a talent for sussing out this sort of thing and, two, I'm sure you can see what I saw the moment Laurent brought me here."

Pauline nodded. "Yes," she said. "That ski pole is mine."

"And I think it's safe to say the only fingerprints on it will be yours, even though you wore gloves when we were skiing yesterday."

"Of course," Pauline said. "I wasn't wearing gloves when I packed the poles or lifted them into the car or the plane."

"It gets worse," Mike said. "Look at this." He stepped aside so Pauline could see the handkerchief lying on the floor beside the bed. The monogrammed initials, PR, were uppermost.

"Yes, that's mine as well. Whoever did this really wants me blamed for it," Pauline said.

"But I, and the other guests, can't overlook the evidence, Pauline," Mike said. "And I know, as they don't, that you really disliked Arnie."

"I disagreed with his work methods and behavior," Pauline said. "That's hardly a motive for murder."

"But you do see the difficulty," Mike said.

"Only if the others see the crime scene," Pauline said, "and they can't be allowed in here. The room must be secured until the police arrive. And you can't seriously believe I had anything to do with this."

"They're my guests," Mike said. "I can't let them be unaware of the danger they may be in."

"Mike," Pauline said. "Be sensible. I'm not a murderer and if I ever decided to become one, I wouldn't use *my* ski pole and leave behind *my* handkerchief with *my* initials conveniently revealed to passers-by."

"I have to do something," Mike said.

"Have you called the police?"

"Like the electrical lines, the phone lines are down," he replied. "I'll keep trying but until then I'll keep this room locked."

"Let me examine the room before you lock it," Pauline said. "There may be some *real* clues here."

Mike hesitated, his expression one of deep concern.

"You can watch me," Pauline said. "That way you'll know I didn't disturb anything."

"Okay," Mike said, "but then I think you need to stay in your room until the police arrive."

As she was expecting something like this, Pauline wasn't surprised. "Very well," she said. "Have Mrs. Pomerleau bring me my meals. That way I needn't upset anyone."

"I thought I might just say you and Arnie were both unwell with flu or something catching like that," Mike said, his embarrassment clear.

"Then you need to put on the TV or music in Arnie's room, to hide the lack of noise from him," Pauline suggested. "My room won't be a problem; I'll be moving about. I like to pace when I think, and this will need lots of pacing."

"The outlets in the bedrooms aren't live," Mike said. "The genny runs only the kitchen and essential services."

Pauline nodded. Her first thought was that meant no hairdryer and a hairdryer was essential to her.

"Then telling them Arnie is in his room isn't going to work. And I need to be searching for clues, not cooped up."

"Who could it be?" Mike asked almost plaintively.

"Well," Pauline said, "if it wasn't you and it wasn't me, that leaves only the other guests and the Pomerleaus."

"The Pomerleaus didn't know him and none of the other guests knew him, other than as an occasional work contact. That surely isn't enough to kill him," Mike said. "I've thought about it, you see."

"Jo was with him most of yesterday and they appeared to me to be high on some drug or other," Pauline said.

"You think he did something, and this is her revenge?" Mike asked.

"I don't think anything yet," Pauline said. "I just know one of us needs to question Jo about yesterday evening and night and if I can't do it, then it has to be you."

"But I can't without telling her he's dead," Mike said.

"Then tell her he's dead but not how he died. See what suggestions that elicits from her."

Mike nodded. "What a mess," he said, shaking his head.

"Interview each one of them alone. Preferably before they've had time to bring their stories into line."

"You need to be there," Mike said. "You're the one with expertise."

"Then we can forget the story of me being ill, but we still

must keep the incriminating evidence from the others so they won't jump to conclusions."

"What will the police say when they get here?" Mike asked. "They won't like it."

"I can refer them to officers in Toronto who will vouch for me," Pauline said. "Now, let me look around and then we'll lock the room."

"Okay, do it."

Her first observation was to the room. She stood inside the doorway, the bed stretched out in front of her with the headboard against the wall on her left and the foot of the bed to her right. Arnie lay naked with his back to her and his head on two pillows, which placed his head at such an angle she could see the whole right side. Beyond the foot of the bed was a wall with built-in closets and a mirrored dresser. The farther wall of the room had long drapes, covering what she was sure would be a large window. They were closed and, as they weren't moving, she knew the window was shut. But was it locked?

Next, Pauline slowly scanned the body, which was laying on the nearer side of the bed and seemed to be lying naturally enough. It was as if he'd been asleep when stabbed and hadn't struggled when the pole's spike went into him. He didn't seem to have moved when the spike went in or after it was removed. Death must have been instantaneous. The ski pole lay on the bed behind him, carefully placed there by the murderer.

Her attention moved to the bed itself. Either Arnie was a restless sleeper or two people had occupied the bed at some time during the night. Based on the afternoon and evening activities, that would suggest Jo. Was there anything to substantiate such a supposition? She looked carefully, peering around the body and into the folds of the cover but there was nothing to be seen from where she stood at the door side of the bed.

The pillows under Arnie's head, two, one on top of the other, had some blood on their covers but not a lot. It confirmed her earlier assumption; he died instantly. The second set of pillows were halfway down the bed and seemed to have been simply dropped there. Unlike the ski pole, there was no obvious care given to their placement.

On the floor, at Mike and Pauline's feet, were Arnie's clothes and shoes. Abandoned as he stripped them off and climbed into bed. Arnie's clothes were there but none belonging to anyone else. Whoever had helped Arnie tangle the cover and pillows had left no trace on this side of the bed.

"I'm moving to the foot of the bed," Pauline said. "Maybe there's more to be seen from there."

Mike followed her as she carefully made her way to the new vantage point. She saw nothing on the wooden floor that they might disturb as they walked but she wanted to be sure.

From here, Arnie looked peaceful, asleep even, for the wound and blood were much less visible. As the body was naked, she could surmise either Arnie didn't wear pajamas to bed, or he hadn't last night because he had company. Nothing new appeared from this point, not on the floor or the bed, so Pauline moved to the other side where she could now see Arnie's face. He looked mildly surprised.

She carefully pushed aside the curtains and examined the window catches. They were closed tightly and the window, like her own, was too high for easy access from outside.

Again, there was no additional evidence of another occupant in the bed. No one had left jewelry or lipstick marks on the bedclothes or anything of that kind. She dropped to her knees and peered under the bed. A suitcase was the only item to be seen and it was probably Arnie's. Checking with Mike, who was silently watching her work, confirmed it didn't belong to the house.

"We'll leave that for the forensics people to examine," Pauline said, "though I'd really like to look inside."

"If it's his case," Mike said, "it will be empty, I should think."

"It should be, I agree," Pauline said, "but it may not be. However, if there'd been anything of interest in it, the person who killed Arnie will have it now. They've been extremely careful to leave no trace of their presence and they wouldn't have missed finding what they came for. If there was something they came for."

"You think this might be a robbery?"

"I don't think anything yet," Pauline said. "It's just one possibility."

"But how would anyone know if Arnie had something of value with him?"

"Maybe he told them," Pauline replied. "There was a lot of loose talk yesterday evening when the drink was taking hold."

"But that means someone here, who has never committed a crime, was so overcome by greed, they went mad and killed Arnie to get something so valuable it was worth taking such a risk."

"I didn't say it was a strong motive," Pauline agreed, "only that it was possible, and we can't ignore it. Anyway, it needn't be something monetary. Arnie knew secrets, like all of us who do audits. Maybe he knew something serious about someone here."

"And they didn't want their life ruined by exposure or blackmail," Mike mused. "Yes, I see what you mean."

Pauline carefully examined the bathroom and any closets that were open. She didn't touch any of the unopened drawers for fear of destroying fingerprints or other evidence the killer may have inadvertently missed.

"Mike," Pauline said, "I'm going to touch Arnie's hand. I'd like to know if he's been dead for hours or only minutes."

"Should we touch the body?"

"That's why I'm telling you and you're going to watch where I touch," Pauline said. "That way we can assure the police anything they find in that one spot is from me."

Mike frowned. "Wait," he said. "If they do think you're the murderer, they'll think you did this to hide something you did when you killed him."

Pauline nodded. "Then you choose the one spot I'll touch. That way, I can't be thought to be obscuring evidence."

Mike nodded. "Okay," he said, approaching the bed. He pointed to Arnie's right forearm that lay on the bed in front of Pauline. "Not the hand, the center of the forearm."

Pauline touched where he'd pointed. "He hasn't been dead long. Certainly not hours, anyway."

"You haven't a thermometer," Mike said. "And the fire is keeping the room warm. How can you be sure?"

"With the electric heating off," Pauline said, "this room is cool, as mine is. Yet I can still feel warmth in his arm. I'd say no more than two hours. However, it is just a guess. The police surgeon will make a better judgment."

"Did you hear anyone in the corridor this morning?"

"I didn't," Pauline said. "Did you?"

Mike shook his head. "I was asleep when Laurent came to find me."

"I don't think there's anything more to be seen here," Pauline said. "I suggest you lock the room door, and we start interviewing the rest of the guests and the Pomerleaus."

"No one is up yet," Mike said.

"Then we can make our plans while we have breakfast," Pauline replied. "I'm starving."

They had the breakfast room to themselves. Surprisingly for Pauline, the death had re-awakened her love of nature and as she ate, she gazed out upon the frozen landscape the storm had left in its wake. She never felt more certain in her faith than when she saw the artistry that nature painted and sculpted daily for everyone's pleasure – if they looked. Sadly, though she couldn't explain it, it seemed all that beauty had to come with violence, whether of the carnivorous kind or just the murderous kind she'd seen today.

The rising sun glowed in the ice that encased every bare tree branch. It shone like luminescent lamps in the shadowy areas between the fir trees. The firs, their needles also encased in ice, glittered like jewels as the sun glinted on the gently swaying boughs. Looking from the window, she was reminded of department stores' Christmas windows; it looked so unreal and yet so vividly real.

"You have experience in this kind of thing," Mike's voice burst in on her reverie. "How do you advise we proceed."

"I suggest we interview Jo first. That way she can't learn anything from the others," Pauline said, turning to watch his expression. "She's the one most likely to have seen Arnie last."

He nodded. "I think so, too. Though some of the others may be able to say what time Arnie and Jo left for bed if they went together."

"They can still tell us that after we've spoken to Jo. It will be a good check on the accuracy of Jo's memory."

"You don't like Jo either, do you?" Mike said wryly.

"I'd say it is Jo who doesn't like me," Pauline replied, "but we were never destined to be friends, it's true."

Mike frowned. "Should you be investigating this? There's some animosity between you and both leading actors in the drama, if I might put it that way."

"If I'd only investigated people I liked down the years," Pauline said, "I wouldn't have investigated anyone. My feelings toward Jo are entirely neutral, as they were toward Arnie. My advice to you about him, and my failure to have a friendship with Jo, aren't predicated on personal animosity. I simply found one a cruel manipulator of truth in the service of personal gain and the other just mean and vindictive."

"Jo has always behaved well toward me," Mike said, though Pauline sensed defensiveness in his body language.

"I've no doubt she does behave well toward you, and to many others," Pauline said. "We all have our favorites in life. I'm sure I'm no different. Now, to work. How can we prevent the others coming down to interrupt when we interview Jo?"

"We can't," Mike said. "Only the first one, if we're quick enough."

"Then it has to be Jo," Pauline replied. "My guess is the older guys, Gilles and Bryan, will be next up. Older people are generally early risers."

"We'll use my office," Mike said. "I'll get a fire lit in there. The generator only supplies the most essential rooms with heat and even then, we only have three days fuel. We have plenty of wood for the fires, though. We won't freeze to death."

"You take photos, don't you?" Pauline asked.

"I sure do," Mike said. "Why?"

"We should take some photos of the crime scene exactly as we saw it. Could you do that?"

"I guess so," Mike said. "But it will take a little time to set up the equipment to do it really well."

Pauline nodded. "Then we need to start right away. Get Laurent started on the fire. We must be ready for when they start waking up."

"I'm surprised some of them haven't come down already," Mike said, as he rose and left the room to find Laurent.

Pauline shook her head in disbelief. After a full day of eating and drinking that they'd all indulged in except Arnie and Jo who were enjoying other pleasures, she doubted they'd see any of the others before lunch time. She planned to rouse Jo and bring her down to breakfast the moment Mike's office was warm enough to sit in.

## 9

# JO'S STORY

PAULINE HAD time to have breakfast, dress, and clean her teeth before she felt the office was ready. When it was, she knocked firmly on the door to Jo's room and ignored all commands from inside for her to go away, which were not expressed in a seemly fashion.

"Mike and I need to speak with you urgently," Pauline said.

There was a low grumbling from inside the room that made Pauline smile. Jo would have enjoyed telling Pauline what she thought of a shared conversation, but Mike was the head of the firm and to an ambitious person, someone to be placated.

"I'll be there in a minute," Jo said.

"I'll wait," Pauline replied.

The grumbling continued but without being quite identifiable as words. Pauline grinned. She wouldn't have liked hearing them if she could hear them. Finally, the door burst open, and Jo marched out, swinging the door violently shut behind her. Pauline was just fast enough to prevent it closing with a bang that might have wakened others.

"We don't want everyone up just yet," Pauline explained in answer to Jo's puzzled expression.

"What's this about?"

"We'll explain when we meet," Pauline said, ushering her along the corridor and down the stairs. "Mike's waiting in his office."

"Why didn't he come up if he wants to see me?"

"Because he's a man and I'm a woman," Pauline said. "You may not have come to your bedroom door dressed to meet your work boss."

They entered the office where Mike was staring out of the window, his expression serious.

"Good morning, Jo."

"Morning, Mike. What's this about?"

Mike looked to Pauline, who said, "Arnie was found dead in his room this morning."

Jo, who had been in the act of sitting, shot bolt upright. "What are you implying? I killed him?"

"I'm not saying anything of the sort," Pauline replied, keeping her temper. Jo was the prickliest customer to deal with, even at work. She seemed to take offense at everything about Pauline.

"We thought you might have been the last person to see Arnie alive," Mike said, before adding hurriedly, "other than the murderer, we mean." He paused briefly before pointing to the tape recorder on his desk, "We're also recording everyone's recollections while they're fresh in their minds. Is that okay?"

Jo's expression didn't lighten, but she did answer, "If you like. I've nothing to hide. Arnie and I were having fun, which isn't easy to do when the party is so small and most of the people are so old." Her cold stare at Pauline signaled her meaning.

"Do you remember what time it was when you last saw him?" Pauline asked, feeling this would be a less provocative question than *where*.

Jo shrugged. "One-ish, I guess." Now she saw the conversation wasn't as pointed as she'd feared, she sat in the chair across the desk from where Mike now sat.

"And at that time there was any indication that anything was wrong?" Pauline asked.

"Are you saying he killed himself?" Jo demanded.

"I'm asking if there was anything that might help explain his death," Pauline responded. "How he died I'll leave to the police and the coroner."

"Jeez," Jo said. "Suicide?" Then she shook her head. "No way," she continued. "He had plans, big plans, for the future."

"So, when you left him, he was very much alive?" Pauline continued.

Jo grinned. "Tired but alive," she said. "Something you wouldn't understand you dried up old crow."

"There's no need for that," Mike said.

Jo laughed. "All day yesterday, we saw her crossing backwards and forwards through the lobby, spying on us. It made us laugh. Back and forth she went, always watching us with her jealous eyes. Envying us our youth and life while she skulks alone, snooping into everyone's doings." She paused and then added sarcastically, to Pauline, "Auditing's the ideal job for you, isn't it? And so is your oh-so-famous criminal snooping. A lifetime of nosing about in the lives of people who *have* lives, to make up for your own empty life of endless disappointment."

'Hey," Mike growled. "Let's keep this focused on Arnie's death, please."

Jo appeared momentarily embarrassed, but her expression quickly returned to its previous stubborn composure.

Pauline had found her jibe hard to bear, for she'd often thought the same but, as calmly as she could, asked, "These big plans you mentioned, were they about Arnie joining Neufeldt or about expanding his own company?"

"He didn't give too many details," Jo said. She seemed to relax now she'd told Pauline what she'd worked herself up to say. Then her expression lightened, "He did have some choice words about you though." She laughed as she remembered.

"He and I worked together," Pauline said. "I didn't approve of his methods."

"We all know that," Jo said.

"How?" Pauline asked.

"Arnie told me, and then Bryan told us all about it last night. He also told us you'd tried to head off Arnie joining Neufeldt."

Pauline looked to Mike for an explanation and was pleased to see he was uncomfortable.

"I talked over what you said earlier with Bryan last night," Mike admitted. "He has years with the company and good judgment. I often consult with him on these kinds of matters. Despite what you all think, he is a valued member of the firm."

"His judgment," Pauline said, through gritted teeth, "is obviously compromised when he has too much to drink."

"It's unfortunate he told the others," Mike said, "but it can't be relevant to what happened."

"Really?" Pauline cried. She wanted to go on but didn't want to alert Jo to the manner of Arnie's death or that this information may have given the murderer the idea of framing herself.

"I see what you mean," Mike said, suddenly seeing the implication of Pauline's question. He had the grace to blush.

"What does she mean?" Jo asked, suspiciously.

"Did you see anyone still up when you left Arnie?" Pauline asked, hoping to divert her attention.

"Now you're suggesting he was murdered," Jo said, refusing to be diverted. "Which is it? Suicide or murder?"

"As I said earlier," Pauline replied. "We'll leave that to the police. Right now, we just want to be sure we don't have someone in the lodge who may be a threat to more of us."

"Jeez," Jo said. "Well, that isn't me. I'm not the murdering kind."

"Which is why we're asking for your help," Mike said, patiently. "Can you walk us through Arnie's movements—" He stopped when Jo broke into his speech with a harsh laugh.

"Little Miss Proper here won't like that," she said.

"We aren't interested in your personal life," Pauline said. "Only what happened to Arnie yesterday evening and into the night. Who he talked to. Who he met. Who might have come to his room after you left. Anything."

Jo's laughter died away, and she was serious. "A lot of it is a bit of a blur," she said.

"Try, please," Mike said. His tone said he was losing patience and had not found her mocking interjection to his taste.

"We stopped dancing for supper," Jo said. She looked at Mike. "You must remember that?"

He nodded and she continued. "Then we all went into the games room, but we couldn't all play. Arnie and I took our drinks back into the lounge. He had some pills, and we took one each. That gave us the energy to dance some more.

You must have seen or heard us," she glanced at Mike for confirmation.

"I did," he said. "I was heading off here," he indicated his office, "where I thought I'd catch up on some papers."

"Later," Jo continued, "we rejoined the others in the lounge. They were sitting around shooting the breeze. Work talk, mainly. Arnie had to go to the bathroom. That's when Bryan told us what you'd told him." Again, she glanced at Mike.

"I'm sorry to learn how little he can be trusted," Mike said.

Jo shrugged. "I don't see the big deal," she said. "Maybe you can enlighten me."

"Later," Mike said. "Then what happened?"

"After Arnie came back from the bathroom," Jo concentrated and then answered, "The talking dribbled away, and people began drifting away. Arnie and I were among the first to go upstairs, I think."

"What time was that?" Pauline asked.

"Maybe eleven-ish? I wasn't looking at the time."

"And when you returned to your own room, you heard and saw nothing?" Mike asked.

"Nothing," Jo replied and then added, "I guess that does mean I was the last to see him alive."

Pauline nodded. A thought had come to her that needed to be followed up the moment Jo was gone. "Well, thanks Jo," she said. "Unless Mike has anything, I have no more questions right now."

Mike shook his head. "None," he said. "Thanks, Jo. We do understand this must have been difficult for you."

Jo shrugged. "It's a shock," she said, "as much as anything. He was very much alive and now to learn he's dead?" She shuddered, then rose to leave the office. At the door, she stopped, "Hey," she said, looking at Pauline, "with a death in the place, shouldn't you be at church chanting *Hail Marys* or something?"

"I'm not Catholic," Pauline replied evenly.

Jo laughed. "And you can't get to church today anyhow. What will God say about your playing hooky?"

"As I was coming here for the weekend, He gave me a rain check," Pauline said, hoping her light tone would be enough to end this distasteful conversation. Her being a churchgoer had come up in a conversation early in her time with Neufeldt and it had given Jo yet another angle of attack.

"What do you think?" Mike asked anxiously once the door was closed.

"There's nothing to show who killed Arnie," Pauline replied "and Jo was there or somewhere near when it happened. We can't rule her out. I suppose she has to be our prime suspect."

"There's evidence pointing to you, though," Mike said.

"Then you must keep that in mind as we proceed," Pauline said. "I, however, don't need to because I know I didn't kill him."

"Who next?"

"If Gilles or Bryan are downstairs, we could talk to them," Pauline said.

"And if they aren't?"

"We need to speak to Laurent Pomerleau as soon as possible," Pauline said. "By his own admission he was alone with Arnie's body before he came to rouse you. Maybe, it was Laurent who killed Arnie."

"I asked him to go out to his truck and call the police on his Citizen's Band radio," Mike said, "but he should be back inside by now. I'll go find him."

Pauline nodded. For the first time, she could see why the CB radio craze had taken hold. With the phones down and the roads closed, it was their only connection to the outside world. Up until now, she'd seen it as the modern-day equivalent of the 1950s amateur radio craze, when slightly strange men, who found it hard to talk to their immediate neighbors, would happily boast about talking about the weather to someone in Tokyo overnight. Now, miles from any modern services and unable to get to them, that radio could be a lifesaver.

## 10

# LAURENT'S STORY

WHILE PAULINE WAITED for Mike to return with either Gilles, Bryan, or Laurent, she gave the matter of motive more thought. If it was Jo, sexual impropriety may be the cause, but who else here had any motive? She, Pauline, was the only one who disliked the man – that she knew of anyhow. And stuck here, miles from anywhere, with the phones out of service, she wasn't going to be able to get background on the others that might suggest a link. Or could she? She had only just realized she could when Mike returned with Laurent in tow.

"Morning, Laurent," Pauline said. "Though we can hardly call it a good one, can we?"

"It's a mess," Laurent said.

"Did you get through to the police?" Pauline asked.

"Sure, but they can't get here any time soon. The roads are feet deep in snow and the snow is covered in ice. They're also busy helping people stuck overnight in their vehicles."

"Then we'll have to put our heads together and solve this ourselves," Pauline said, smiling.

"You're right there," Laurent said. "Catrina doesn't want to spend another night here if there's a murderer loose."

Pauline nodded. "I understand how she feels."

"Pauline wanted to hear how you found Arnie's body, Laurent," Mike said, "and I should warn you, we're recording everyone's recollections."

"Fine," Pomerleau said, "I've nothing to hide. There's not much to tell. I thought I heard a noise upstairs. It sounded like wind was blowing through something that was open. I came up and saw Mr. Hamilton's door was open. When I got to the door, I saw he'd been stabbed in the head and I came to find you, Mike."

"And we returned to the room together," Mike said, addressing Pauline. "I pulled the door closed and came for you while Laurent went to call the police."

"You heard the noise upstairs from the kitchen?" Pauline asked Laurent.

Laurent shook his head. "No. When the genny's running, there's not enough power for the electric wall heaters. The fire in the lobby is the only way of getting heat throughout the whole building. I came into the lobby to light the fire there. That's when I heard it."

"It wasn't just the wind in the fireplace chimney you heard?"

"It sounded like it came from upstairs," Laurent said.

"When you went upstairs, did you find anything open?" Pauline asked.

"Nothing," he said.

"Not even the windows in Arnie Hamilton's room?"

"Nothing," Laurent replied.

"Then what was the noise? Can you describe it?"

"It only lasted a few seconds. I thought it was the wind," he replied, "blowing through a narrow opening, a window cracked open or maybe the storm had opened a hole in the roof or wall."

"Could it have been a squeaky door closing?" Pauline asked.

"Could be," Laurent said. "I didn't think so at the time."

"And Arnie's room door was open?"

"Yes. I said so."

"I'm sure you've thought of this already," Pauline said, "and the police certainly will. Had you any reason to want him dead?"

"The first time I met him was yesterday when he arrived," Laurent said. "We barely exchanged two words since then."

Pauline nodded. "You see what I'm getting at, I'm sure. One possible explanation of all this is you stabbed him."

Laurent looked uncomfortable but answered, "It was the first thing I thought – *they'll say I did it*. But I didn't and I don't see how anyone could prove I did."

"You didn't handle that ski pole at any time yesterday, did you?" Mike asked, alarmed.

"I brought in all the luggage," Laurent said. "It doesn't mean anything."

"That's true," Mike said, brightening.

"Did you enter the room?" Pauline continued.

"I took a step inside, thinking it might not be what it looked like," Laurent said. "I saw at once it was exactly what I'd thought and backed out."

"You didn't touch him?"

Laurent shook his head. "He was dead. There was no need to check his pulse or anything."

"Did you see or hear anyone moving about at any time, before, during, or after your discovery?"

"Only the noise that brought me upstairs."

"I wish we could find out what that was," Pauline said. "That might give us a clue. You're sure it was upstairs?"

"I thought so, that's why I came up," Laurent said. "That's all I can say about it. I haven't heard it since."

"Thanks, Laurent," Mike said, when it was clear Pauline had no further questions. "Your information may help us nail this killer. And, please, it will help the investigation a lot if you don't tell anyone what you saw."

Laurent nodded. "I hope it does help or Catrina will have me driving us home tonight and I'd rather not move until the roads are plowed."

"Speaking of Catrina," Mike said, "would you ask her to come and talk to us. Tell us what she saw yesterday."

"If you want your guests fed," Laurent said, "you'll let her get on. She's pretty busy right now, what with the power being out earlier and not everything available."

"Understandably," Mike said. "After everything's done will be fine."

"Laurent," Pauline said, as he was heading for the door, "could you show me how to work your CB radio? I'd like to talk to a police inspector I know well in Toronto. He could help with background on Arnie."

"Sure," Laurent said. "Now?"

"Is your truck outside? I probably need my ski clothes on because it will take time."

"It's inside the garage," Laurent said, "but you will need to be wrapped up well. It's minus thirty out there and the garage is not much warmer."

"Then I'll come and find you soon," Pauline replied. "Thanks."

Laurent left the office, leaving them to stare at his retreating figure making his way down the hall.

"We don't have any other suspects, do we?" Mike asked.

"No and without researching the backgrounds of everyone here, I'm not sure we can learn much more," Pauline replied. "We must interview everyone, though," she added. "Let's see who has made it down to breakfast."

"Wouldn't it be better to call your Toronto police friend early?" Mike asked. "We may get information back today if it's available."

Pauline considered. She was torn between interviewing everyone before they could talk and align their stories and calling Inspector Ormiston.

"You're right," she said. "He can be researching background while we interview the others. I'll go and dress for the outdoors."

# 11

# INSPECTOR ORMISTON HELPS OUT

LAURENT WAS RIGHT, her wait for Inspector Ormiston to be brought to a radio was a very cold one. The CB radio, unfortunately, was in the truck and its microphone was attached to it by a short cable; there was no way it could reach the house where fires were now burning in every hearth.

It had taken some time to raise Toronto police on the radio and now it was taking time for them to find Ormiston. With the garage doors closed, they couldn't run the truck for fear of the exhaust fumes. She could only huddle herself into a small ball inside the cab and hope for an early release.

"Miss Riddell." The radio speaker crackled into life. "How nice to hear from you."

Reception wasn't good, being inside the garage probably had a lot to do with that, and his words, though understandable, were almost drowned out by the steady thump of the generator's diesel engine, which was running in a building just outside the farther end of the garage. The sound reverberated through the building. She hoped he could hear her.

"It's nice of you to say so, Inspector," Pauline said,

speaking slowly. "Please speak slowly and clearly because we have a diesel generator running that makes it hard for me to hear you. Can you hear me well?"

When Ormiston confirmed he could, Pauline said, "I'm calling to ask a favor."

He laughed. "Miss Riddell, you *only* call when you want a favor."

She smiled. That was true but the assistance she'd provided him in return on a number of occasions should mean the obligations were equal.

"I don't like to be a nuisance, Inspector, but I have a list of names I need background on."

"And Toronto Police have nothing better to do," he said, but she was sure she could hear a smile in his voice.

"Exactly so," Pauline said. "Have you pen and paper?"

"I have. Fire away."

She gave him the names of the people at the lodge and after he'd read it back, told him why it was necessary.

"You've informed the local police?"

"We radioed them earlier," Pauline said, "but they won't get here for days. Not until after they've located and rescued all the stranded motorists and the roads are plowed."

"Meanwhile you're stuck in a cottage with a murderer," Ormiston said. "Nice."

"I don't think we're in any danger," Pauline said. "Whatever the motive, it can hardly include the rest of us."

"You must hope so, anyhow," Ormiston said.

"I can't see how it could be otherwise," Pauline replied. "None of us know each other well, except as work colleagues. And the victim wasn't even that."

"How will I get in touch if I learn anything?" Ormiston asked.

"Unfortunately, the radio is in a truck outside so no one

will pick up," Pauline said. "I'll call you after lunch and again after supper if that works for you?"

With this agreed, Pauline hung up the microphone, switched off the radio, and returned to the house and the next interviews.

## 12

# JOHN'S STATEMENT

"SHOULDN'T we wait for the police before we provide statements?" John asked, as he entered the office.

Mike explained that Pauline had experience in solving murders and that was why he'd asked her to help investigate the death of Arnie Hamilton. He added that they were recording the conversation.

John nodded. "They told me about the recording when I came down to an early brunch."

"You like to sleep late?" Pauline asked, smiling.

He grinned. "I do on a day off when I know there's nothing to get up for. There was no way we were going skiing after the ice storm last night."

"True enough," Mike said. "Anyhow, now you are up, maybe you can help us with what you were doing last night and anything you might know that could shed light on what happened."

John shrugged. "It won't be much. I was with everyone in the lobby and games room last night and then I went to bed. I got up, had a shower, and came down to be ushered in here. That's it, in one sentence." He paused, grinned and continued, "Sorry, in two sentences. Auditors should be precise"

"Did you know Arnie?" Pauline asked.

"Never met him until I arrived here," John said. "I spoke to him once or twice on Friday evening and again on Saturday but that was all."

"What did you talk about?" Mike asked.

"On Friday, we talked about who I was and who he was, what I did and what he did," John replied. "On Saturday, we talked about the quality of the snow and our good luck to be back inside when the ice storm arrived."

"You've never come in contact with him through work?" Pauline asked.

He shook his head. "No, not at all. I know he's been around years, he told me so, but I'm too new to have met him or even heard of him. I think he was a bit disappointed at that, actually."

Pauline smiled. "Arnie did like to think he was the center of the universe, or at least our small part of it."

"I got that impression," John said, grinning. "I also got the impression he didn't rate me as an important contact to be developed."

Pauline laughed. "He was very open and direct in his dealings with others. If you didn't impress, he dropped you."

"I understand you worked with him," John said.

"Once," Pauline replied. "I didn't impress him either."

"Can we get back to last night?" Mike asked. "Did you hear anything when you went to bed or during the night, John?"

John considered for a moment. "Nothing but that's because I'd had more than my usual to drink. I rarely drink, you see. I slept like a log."

"Did you hear or see anything last night that might help?" Pauline asked.

"I'm sure you saw what I saw," John replied, "and I know you've spoken to Jo, so I won't waste time on that. I did see Hamilton and Bryan in a one-on-one that looked intense. That's it, I'm afraid." He paused and asked, "Was his death because of the drink and drugs?"

"You thought he'd taken something, did you?" Pauline asked.

"I'm not an expert on drugs but I think we all thought so," John replied. "Didn't you?"

"We aren't speculating about what killed him," Mike said. "The police and their pathologist can decide that. We're just trying to capture everyone's recollections while they're still fresh. It may be days before the police can be here in person."

"Well, I think I've told you all I know," John said, "and it won't help you or the police, I'm afraid."

"You never know," Pauline said. "Sometimes the smallest thing can be just what an investigator needs."

John grinned. "Like in the movies where the murderer accidentally reveals they've held a grudge against the victim from years before, when everyone believed they didn't."

Pauline was momentarily surprised. Then she saw his smile and realized she was being teased. "Quite so, John, but everyone knows I didn't like or admire Arnie Hamilton."

"They were talking about it as I passed the breakfast room," he said. "I couldn't resist."

When he was gone, Mike said, "I'll never trust Bryan again."

"He too had more to drink than was good for him," Pauline reminded Mike.

"But how many company secrets has he revealed to

others when he's had too much to drink," Mike replied. "If nothing else, this incident has alerted me to a danger I didn't know we had."

"You must have known he was resentful about missing out on the top job, though," Pauline said, puzzled.

"When these things happen to us, we're all angry to some extent," Mike replied. "But he stayed and seemed to be over his pique. I've always gone to him for advice, based on his long experience with the firm, and his advice was always good when I consulted him."

"We can't let this color our opinion when we interview Bryan," Pauline said. "We have to stay neutral, or he'll clam up and we'll get nothing."

"Maybe we should leave him to last, then," Mike replied. "At this moment, I could kill him..." He stopped and then said, "Just a turn of phrase, not a threat."

"I'll go see who's in the breakfast room," Pauline said.

The breakfast room was almost silent when she entered. Either the drinking of the previous evening had them all hungover or the knowledge someone had died was depressing them. Jo stirred a coffee, staring into the cup like she could see clouds in it, as the old song said. John was brighter, happily heaping peameal bacon, scrambled eggs, and hash browns onto a large plate. His appetite at least wasn't dimmed by an alcoholically induced sour stomach. Saul Monkhouse was pushing oatmeal around in a bowl as though it was a form of exercise and Tom, like John, was finishing a large plate of everything on the food counter. There were times, Pauline thought, when young men were positively unlikeable simply because they were so healthy and young man-ish.

"Mike and I have captured Jo and John's recollections of yesterday and last night," Pauline said. "Saul or Tom, would either of you like to be the first to tell us what you can remember?"

Tom pushed back his chair. "Why not," he said. "I don't know anything so the sooner that's said, the sooner I can get on with the day. How did Arnie die, by the way?"

"That decision is best left to the experts," Pauline said, as she led the way out of the room and down the corridor to Mike's office.

"You must have some idea, though?" Tom said.

"It's best we don't speculate," Pauline said as they entered the office.

"Hi, Tom," Mike said, "take a seat." He explained about the purpose of the interview and the tape.

"Yeah, yeah," Tom replied, nodding. "John and Jo told me all that. What do you want to know? Did I kill him?"

"Did you?" Mike asked, surprised at Tom's levity.

"Of course not," Tom said. "I'm just a bit nervous, I guess. Sorry for that."

"What can you tell us about yesterday that you might have seen but we and the others didn't?" Pauline asked.

"Nothing really," Tom said, frowning in concentration. "I was with Arnie and the others on the lake, but we were going too hard for conversation. Then we came inside just as the storm arrived and had drinks. There was a lot of banter, you'll remember, and then pool and darts. Nothing happened there that we all didn't see."

"After lunch was different," Mike said.

Tom nodded. "The drink was taking a hold by then and the group broke up, particularly when Jo and Arnie began dancing. They looked a bit spaced-out, to be honest, but maybe it was just the booze."

"Where were you and the others?" Pauline asked.

"You know where we were. You were there. We were in

the games room, mainly, with some time spent watching hockey on TV. Thank God we have the generator for today, I say. If we had no electricity at all, we'd murder each other by supper time."

Mike said, "Only some outlets will be working, and we'll have to use the electricity sparingly to make the diesel fuel last."

Tom grimaced. "I didn't mean we'd murder each other literally, of course, but it will create tension if there's nothing to do. I can't help thinking that's what happened to Arnie, tensions, I mean. Was he murdered?"

"Why do you think he might be?" Pauline asked.

"Oh, just the way it is with guys and drink. He got the girl, and we didn't. He's a successful company owner and wasn't shy telling us we were just wage-slaves. He didn't mince words when he'd had a few."

"Did you resent him?" Mike asked.

"A little. Like I said, he wasn't pleasant when he was drunk," Tom replied. "At least, not to me and others."

"What others?" Pauline asked.

"It's best you ask them. I was angry at his implied opinion of me but maybe the others weren't."

"You didn't fight with him?" Mike said.

"Is that how he died?"

"I'm just asking if you were angry enough to fight with him."

Tom shook his head. "No. I just kept out of his way. He'd already told us he had a black belt in judo and karate by then. My guess is that was more of his BS but who knows."

"In the evening," Pauline said, nudging him back to the purpose of the interview.

Tom shrugged. "More of the same, really. Arnie and Jo

dancing to rock music and the rest of us drinking in the games room and watching hockey."

"What time did you go upstairs?" Mike asked.

"I'm not sure exactly. After the game finished. Like all hockey fans, I hang on to the end 'cos that's when the real action happens."

"So, after eleven-ish," Mike said. "Did you hear or see anything that might shed light on what happened?"

"Nothing. Arnie and Jo had come up earlier and both their room doors were closed. I heard voices in Arnie's room and assumed it was them. I crashed on the bed and didn't wake until morning."

"Nothing else happened that struck you as odd?" Pauline asked.

"Nothing," Tom replied. "Nothing at all."

They thanked him and he returned to the breakfast room with the message to ask Saul to come to the office.

"I think we'll hear the same thing from Saul, Gilles, and Bryan," Mike said. "Nobody knows anything."

"Probably but you never know what people see or hear until you ask."

## 13

# SAUL AND GILLES

BUT SAUL WAS EQUALLY BAFFLED by the events as Tom. His story was essentially the same in every detail.

"Tom said Arnie had been unpleasant to him," Pauline asked. "Was he unpleasant to you?"

"He wasn't unpleasant," Saul said. "He was just one of those guys who likes to brag, not understanding it makes others feel uncomfortable."

"Maybe he did understand, and he enjoyed making people uncomfortable," Mike said.

Saul nodded, grinning. "Yeah, he probably did, but it was just his way. You'd have to be very insecure to be upset at it. Every locker room has a dozen guys like that in it."

Mike laughed. "I'm not sure Tom plays team sports."

"He *is* a bit of a wuss," Saul said, grinning even more broadly. "Anyhow, you know what I mean."

"You heard and saw nothing upstairs or during the night that struck you as odd?" Pauline asked.

Saul shook his head. "The wind was making so much noise around my corner room, I'd have missed World War Three."

"Well, thanks for helping, Saul. If you remember anything, you will let us know, won't you?" Mike said. "Ask Gilles to come and talk to us."

"I told you so," Mike said, when Saul was gone. "And I don't think it's because they got together and aligned their stories."

Pauline nodded. "My own story is much the same. I heard the wind and the ice rattling on the roof and windows several times during the night but no murders being committed. I didn't even hear Jo leave Arnie's room and return to her own, let alone someone else entering and murdering him."

Before Mike could reply, Gilles entered the room.

"Morning," he said, plunking himself down in the chair apposite Pauline and Mike.

Pauline smiled. Gilles always reminded her of a bear but on a vacation morning with no work to attend, his hair and beard, normally restrained, looked positively shaggy.

"Good morning, Gilles," Pauline said. "I've no doubt the others have briefed you."

He nodded. "And I'm okay with it, recording and all."

"I know we were together much of yesterday evening," Mike said. "Your preliminary findings on the Renseiller audit are disturbing. Now, can you tell us anything you saw or heard before or after our discussion?"

"There's not a lot to tell," Gilles said. "Before we came in here to talk, everything seemed normal. I don't remember anything unusual at all. Then after we talked, I went back to my room to make notes on what we'd said."

"What time would that be?" Pauline asked.

"What time did I go upstairs?" Gilles repeated thoughtfully. "I don't exactly know but about nine-thirty, I'd guess. What would you say, Mike?"

"I'd say that was about right. Did you hear anything during the night?"

"The wind and ice pellets occasionally," Gilles said. "It was a wild night. I heard people coming up to their rooms around eleven. Afterwards, nothing. Out like a light, I was."

"What about early this morning?" Pauline asked.

Gilles shook his head. "I slept until I heard people coming down for breakfast."

With no further questions, Mike and Pauline thanked him and asked him to send Bryan their way.

# 14

## BRYAN'S VIEW

"ARE we ready to hear from Bryan without jumping down his throat?" Mike asked, grinning.

Pauline only had time to nod before Bryan entered the room.

"Hi, Bryan," Mike said, smiling.

Pauline thought Bryan would see the tautness in Mike's smile and neck muscles and see right through this attempt at friendliness.

She smiled and said, "Good morning, Bryan." She hoped she looked more relaxed than Mike did.

"Morning," Bryan said, taking the chair offered. He didn't look happy. "I know what you want and you're recording it so don't bother with all that. I've nothing to hide so I'm happy to tell you about my non-part in the events."

From his almost word-perfect repetition of what the others had said, Pauline knew the talk in the breakfast room had been comprehensive. They'd learn nothing new from this interview.

"We're hoping if we collect everyone's statements while

it's fresh in our minds, it will help the police when they get here," Mike said. "That's all, really."

"So, you two have recorded your own statements, have you?"

"Not yet," Mike admitted, glancing at Pauline.

"Exactly, Mike," Bryan said. "You've let the only person with a known grudge against Arnie listen in on everyone's stories before she gives her version of events. Not wise, I think you'll discover."

"I had no reason to harm Arnie," Pauline said. "Though it is true I didn't like his methods and I didn't think we should have him join us in Neufeldt."

"So you say," Bryan replied, "but, I repeat, you're the only one who had any connection with him, you didn't like him, and yet you have the opportunity to tailor your statement to fit in with everyone else's. I call that a tad suspicious, if not something worse."

"I asked Pauline to help me out," Mike said, "because she has expertise in this kind of thing."

"Her expertise didn't extend to recording her own statement before hearing others', which a strictly honest investigator might have done in these circumstances."

"It's true," Pauline said, hoping to head this off before it became acrimonious, "I should have thought of that. I dived in without a thought-out plan and that was wrong of me. However, we're where we are, and the police will interview us all when they get here. They can decide if there are holes in my evidence."

"I, and the others, intend to see they do," Bryan replied. "Now, here's what I remember seeing and hearing..."

His statement was much as the others. He'd played pool and darts, drunk beer and Scotch, watched hockey on TV, saw Arnie and Jo go upstairs before retiring himself. He hadn't heard Jo and Arnie as he'd passed Arnie's room door but then his hearing wasn't so good nowadays. Thanks to the alcohol, he'd slept through until morning without even hearing the storm.

"One last thing, Bryan," Pauline said. "You were having an intense discussion with Arnie earlier in the evening. Can you tell us what that was about?"

Bryan looked as if he was going to refuse, then said, "He and I had a run in a few years back. He made a snide remark earlier in the day and I put him straight on how we were going to behave for this weekend."

"He was okay with that?" Mike asked.

"Eventually we agreed on an acceptable working arrangement."

"That didn't lead to anything more unpleasant?" Pauline asked.

"If you mean, did I kill him, no, I didn't," Bryan said, sharply.

Seeing they wouldn't get anything more from him, Mike and Pauline thanked him for his help.

"Will the police get here today?" Bryan asked, as he rose to leave.

"Probably not," Mike said.

"Then we, your other guests, suggest Miss Riddell stay in her room and the room is kept locked overnight. If she wants to leave her room, we want one of the younger men to escort her to wherever she's going."

"What?" Mike cried, astonished.

"You heard," Bryan said. "She's the only one with a known motive and who knows what other motives she might have."

"You can't be serious, Bryan," Mike said. "Pauline is half

your size and a middle-aged woman. She's no physical threat to anyone here."

"I'm not so young as I was and Arnie was stronger than any of us, but he fell asleep. As we all will tonight. It doesn't matter how young or strong you are when you're asleep you're a sitting duck. Locked in is the least we expect, to be honest."

Before Mike could reply, Pauline held up her hand. "I'm okay with it, Mike," she said. "During the day, you and I can work together. Later, I'll read in my room. You can lock the door – but you keep possession of the key."

"It's ridiculous," Mike began, but, seeing Pauline's expression, continued, "but if it will keep the peace until the police arrive, and because Pauline agrees to accept it, we will do as Pauline suggests. Does that meet you and the others' needs?"

"I'm sure it will," Bryan said. "Understand this, both of you, we're all resolved on this course of action. We've thought about it, and Miss Riddell is the only possible murderer." He left the room as angry as he'd entered.

"Well," Pauline said, "at least we know where we stand."

"I'm not happy about where we're standing though. I can't believe what they're saying."

"You pointed out that it was my ski pole at the start," Pauline reminded him, "and we discussed my keeping apart even then. They're only saying what we talked about two hours ago. We shouldn't be surprised."

"I pointed out the ski pole because it was too obvious to be ignored and I thought you staying apart would be wise for your own safety."

Pauline nodded. "The murderer has used the information you gave Bryan, and the murderer has cleverly shared some more details with them, to play on that same idea. My motive is the only one that's obvious and he or she wants me under suspicion until the police arrive. They clearly hope it will set the police following that path and he or she will continue to feed in the evidence to keep it going."

"The murderer's motive is hidden, that's true," Mike said. "I can't imagine what it is." He paused, and then asked, "What evidence?"

"I don't know yet," Pauline said, "but you can be sure it exists. This is a carefully worked out plan."

"How can it be?" Mike said. "The murderer can't have known you and Arnie would both be here until just a day ago because that's when Arnie confirmed it to me."

"I knew Arnie was invited a week ago," Pauline said. "Presumably the murderer knew that too and the plan was made then. If Arnie didn't come, the plan would be canceled or changed." She sighed. "Here's hoping Inspector Ormiston can shed some light on this puzzle when we talk with him after lunch."

# 15

## CATRINA'S STATEMENT

Inspector Ormiston, however, when Pauline finally got through to him on the CB radio, had nothing very exciting to say.

"It's early days, Miss Riddell," he said, when Pauline voiced her disappointment. "You only asked at eight o'clock this morning and we've hardly gotten into our stride. You might also remember it's Sunday, so we have only the weekend crew in the station. I may have more for you later today. Call again around six."

Pauline thanked him and ended the call.

As she exited the truck, Mike, who'd been listening to the call, said, "I hope he does have something later so we can find a better suspect than you."

"I share that sentiment," Pauline said, smiling, "because it will make for interesting times at work next week if we don't have a solution, particularly if the police don't find one either."

They walked back into the house together. In the lobby, Pauline paused to observe her fellow guests glaring at her from the games room. She met their gaze without flinching, hoping she'd see on one face a hint of triumph that might point her to the real murderer. She couldn't see anything of that kind from Jo, Tom, Saul, Gilles, or Bryan who were watching to see where she went. John was leaning over the pool table, concentrating on his shot and seemingly unaware of the small drama going on behind him.

From the corner of her eye, Pauline saw Catrina Pomerleau stacking dishes in the kitchen.

"We still need to interview Mrs. Pomerleau," she said to Mike.

"I can't think she had anything to do with it," he replied. "I'm not sure she even spoke to him."

Pauline didn't mention the conversation she'd heard the evening before. Instead, she said, "She may not have spoken to him this weekend but that doesn't mean at some time in her life she didn't have dealings with Arnie. And I doubt any woman who had dealings with Arnie would remember him fondly."

"Hey, that's not fair," Mike said. "You've no reason to suggest that."

"My dealings with him were purely platonic," Pauline replied, "and I had no wish to repeat them. I can't know how his personal dealings with women have been, it's true, but I have grave doubts about the happiness they might have caused."

Mike frowned. "You're right about talking to Catrina," he said, nodding. "We can't know if they ever met. She isn't likely to admit it, though, if what you suggest is true."

"If Inspector Ormiston finds a link between her and Arnie that she hasn't revealed, it will be a strong indication of possible wrongdoing."

"You head off to the office. I'll ask her to join us," Mike said.

However, when they met with her, Catrina assured them she'd never met Hamilton, not in the past and not even this weekend. Her forays out from the kitchen hadn't brought them into contact at all.

"You didn't hear or see anything that could shed light on what happened?" Pauline asked.

"No," Catrina said. "We did stay over because of the weather but our room is above the garage. It's too far from the house to hear anything. Anyway, the storm was too loud."

"You didn't look out of a window during the night?" Mike asked. He grinned, "You see how desperate we are for a clue."

Catrina smiled. "I wish I could help but even if I had, the bedroom windows look out to the lake not across to the house. I took sleeping pills to help me sleep and I was out like a light the moment my head touched the pillow."

"Have you met anyone here before?" Pauline asked. "Maybe at college when you were younger?"

Catrina shook her head. "Some of the guests I recognize because they've been here before, but I don't really know anyone," she said. She paused, and when she saw Pauline was still waiting for an answer about her time at college, she added, "though if it was someone from my college days, I might not recognize them now. Or they me, I should think."

"Did you go to college in the south?" Mike asked.

"I trained as a teacher in Toronto," Catrina replied, "but I came back home right after, and I've hardly ever visited the city since. I didn't like it when I was there, and I find even short visits more than enough for me."

There seemed nothing else to say, so they thanked her, and she returned to the kitchen.

"You know what bothers me," Pauline said, frowning.

"No. What?"

"I know they all had way too much to eat and drink but every one of them says how well they slept. Did you sleep well?"

Mike considered. "Not really," he said. "The storm shook the windows and doors a lot and it woke me every time."

"I was the same. If the murder hadn't happened and we'd been talking about last night at breakfast, I would have said I didn't sleep at all. I was awakened so often by the noise."

"It is odd. If this was a book, I'd say they were all in it together, like *Murder on the Orient Express*."

Pauline laughed. "That's the story I was thinking of too."

"There couldn't be anything like that here, though, could there?"

"I don't think so," Pauline replied. "The coincidence of them all having a reason to kill Arnie and all working in this one firm is too much to be sensible."

"Coincidences do happen in life," Mike said, "and it could be something work-related."

"Well, it isn't anything recent and most of them, Jo, Tom, and John, in particular, are too young to have been injured by something Arnie had done in the far past."

"Still," Mike said, slowly, "their insistence of a good night's sleep is odd."

"I think they just don't want to offer anything up as a hostage to fortune," Pauline replied. "The moment they say they might have heard or seen something the police will never let them go. And if it turns out to be nothing, they see themselves being blamed for wasting police time. No, I think they're just protecting themselves."

"Hey," Mike said. "I had another thought. What about the book, *And Then There Were None*?"

Pauline laughed. "If you remember that rightly, you'll realize you've just implicated yourself for it was the owner of the house who was murdering all the guests."

Mike grinned sheepishly. "Forget I said that."

"I will and you have to hope the local detectives aren't fans of mystery books and movies," Pauline said.

"You can give me a character reference," Mike responded, and then asked, "What are your plans for the rest of the afternoon?"

"First, I'm going to add my own recorded statement and then, if you don't mind, I'll take the recordings upstairs to my room and listen to them," Pauline said. "Maybe something will jump out that I missed when we were talking to our witnesses."

"What will you say in your statement?"

"What I just told you a few moments ago. I didn't sleep well because of the storm. Sadly, even with that to help me, I still didn't hear anyone moving about at any of the times I was awake."

"I'll come with you," he said, "and add my own statement to the record."

"I'll ask you questions," Pauline said, as they made their way back to Mike's office, "and you can ask me questions. That way, nothing should get forgotten."

## 16

# GATHERING BACKGROUND

Safely in her room, Pauline sat with the cast iron door of the woodburning stove open so she could enjoy the glowing embers as she listened to each recording, pausing and repeating where necessary, looking for inconsistencies or meaningful inflexions in the voices. After two hours, she'd discovered precisely nothing new. The only two people who seemed to be likely suspects were Catrina, because the conversation Pauline had overheard contradicted what she said in her statement about not knowing any of the guests at the lodge, and Jo who was clearly the last person to see Arnie alive and had the easiest access to his bedroom.

Of the two, only Jo knew Pauline and might dislike Pauline enough to implicate her in the murder, as the murderer clearly had. Catrina had no reason to point the finger at Pauline and was unlikely to know Pauline's ski poles from any of the others. Jo had always resented Pauline's presence in the company. Pauline suspected it was because until Pauline's arrival, Jo had been the only woman in the firm and was therefore getting the attention being focused on 'women in the financial industry' that was so popular now.

However, other than unpleasantness during their love-making, Pauline knew of no reason why Jo would kill Arnie, whereas Catrina clearly disliked someone here in the lodge and Arnie was the closest fit in age and personality. Bryan and Mike were too old, Tom and John were too young, and Saul was a nonentity. Gilles, of course, she'd known and worked for across several years and could be discounted.

As the light outside the window faded away, Pauline heard steps in the corridor outside her door. There was a knock.

"Yes?" she called.

"It's Mike and Catrina, Pauline. We have your supper."

"Wait a minute," Pauline said. The door was locked from outside, but Pauline had wedged a chair under the door handle to ensure it couldn't be easily opened from outside should someone other than Mike get hold of a key. She may be locked in, but she knew the murderer wasn't in her bedroom and that's how she intended it to stay.

When the chair was removed, she said, "You can come in now."

The key turned in the lock and the door opened. Catrina smiled hesitantly as she picked the tray off the floor and handed it over. "Is there anything you'd like to drink?"

Pauline noted the bottled water on the tray. "Water will be fine for now. I'd like tea after."

"I'll bring it up in an hour, shall I?"

Pauline shook her head. "Mike and I are going to use the CB radio at six so if you make it for then, I can bring it up with me."

Catrina nodded and closed the door. Pauline heard Mike

turn the key, locking it once again. Pauline replaced the chair under the door handle.

Pauline had finished her meal and was jotting down additional questions for Inspector Ormiston when she heard Mike's knock on the door.

"I'll be with you in a second," she said, hastily dressing in warmer clothes. She hadn't liked to put on her outdoor clothes before; she thought sweating unladylike.

By the time she was ready, the door was unlocked and open. Pauline stepped out with the tray to carry back to the kitchen. Before setting off, Pauline said, "Please lock the door behind us. I don't want any unpleasant pranks played while I'm out of the room."

Even with another layer of outdoor coats, the temperature in the garage was bone-chilling. Unfortunately, the thick gloves she was wearing made inserting the key in the ignition to get power to the electrics and the radio operating, clumsy, which meant everything took longer. Finally, she heard Ormiston's voice.

"Good evening, Miss Riddell. You haven't frozen to death yet, then."

"I will if we stay chatting too long, Inspector," Pauline replied. "Have you any news?"

"Some but the details are too much for memory and notetaking, I fear. Do you have a fax machine there?"

Pauline looked at Mike, who nodded and gave Ormiston the number to send the details to, adding, "But right now our phone lines are down so we can't send or receive anything." He handed the microphone back to Pauline.

"Is there anything that stands out?" Pauline asked. "Anything we should know right away?"

Ormiston laughed. "Some. The victim wasn't a popular

man by all accounts. He had made many enemies in his professional and personal life but maybe you knew that."

"I didn't know the extent of it," Pauline said. "Is there anything about the others that's noteworthy?"

"Nothing that would suggest murder," Ormiston replied. "Mr. Forrester was involved in a student demo and arrested. It never came to court. Ms. Edwards has been questioned about minor drug-related incidents but never charged with anything. Mr. Monkhouse has enough parking tickets to paper a fair-sized room. Mr. O' Connell is a well-respected man without a blemish on his character so far as we, the police, know. Your Mr. Beresford came to Canada only eight months ago and we're still waiting for information back from the US authorities."

"As you say, Inspector, on the surface nothing to suggest murder. What about the Pomerleaus?"

"The police up there are a bit busy right now," Ormiston replied. "I'm still waiting to learn more about them."

"When can we call tomorrow?" Pauline asked.

"Same arrangement as today, Miss Riddell," Ormiston replied. "Lunch and supper times you'll find me. You need to understand, however, this isn't a high priority for me or my people; we'll only be working on it between other cases. And, so there's no misunderstanding, I'll be sending the police up there the information I'm sharing with you."

"I quite understand," Pauline replied. "Who are you sending it to? I could talk to them when we have our phones restored."

"Inspector Etienne LaPlante," Ormiston said, and gave Pauline his phone number.

Back in the house, Catrina had a pot of tea made and hot buttered bannocks to warm her. Pauline accepted both gratefully. Toronto's winters were only slightly colder and snowier than those of northern England but here in Canada's wintry north, the cold was more than her body could take. Whenever she ventured north in winter, she thought that maybe a little more plumpness would help.

Pauline and Mike took their hot drinks to the office and closed the door. When they were seated, Pauline, who'd noticed Mike's dark expression since hearing about his work colleagues' police records, said, "Don't change your opinion of your friends and work colleagues based on anything you heard from Inspector Ormiston. Nobody looks well in the authorities' eyes and we are all more than the records show."

"That's all very well," Mike said, grimly, "but sometimes that 'more than' means murderer, or drug addict, or another undesirable trait."

Frowning, Pauline said, "Nevertheless, these people work with us and have treated us as colleagues. They didn't ask for *our* police records before they did that. You must put whatever you learn here aside when we return to our previous lives."

Mike nodded. "I noticed you didn't ask for their file on me," he said. "Why are you so sure I'm not the murderer?"

"I'm not sure," Pauline said, "and when the police do get here, they'll see that gap in my investigation. They can fill in your details by themselves. Should I have asked?"

Mike grinned. "I did some pretty stupid stuff as a kid," he said. "Saul has parking tickets, though who doesn't in Toronto. I have speeding tickets."

Pauline laughed. "Remember that when you eventually get to read the files. Now I'm returning to my room to ponder."

Laurent Pomerleau had piled more split logs for the wood burning heater outside her bedroom door which Pauline and Mike carried inside before Mike left, locking the door behind him. The heater's iron shell radiated a pleasant warmth that was amplified when Pauline opened the door so the fiery glow inside could be seen. She plunked herself on the room's chaise-longue style couch and stared into the flames while her mind examined every item Ormiston had provided.

It didn't take long. She remembered more details than she'd recorded in her notes at the time, that was true, but they were so insignificant that they were re-assuring. Nevertheless, she added them now. Despite Mike's fears, to her more experienced eyes, far from being drug taking and parking violating brigands, her colleagues were a rather dull set.

It's true, her ears had pricked up when Ormiston mentioned drugs but to a reasonable person Jo just looked like she was in the wrong place at the wrong time, though it was on two separate occasions. Did having friends who liked marijuana make her a murderer? Pauline thought not, though she was reluctant to let the matter drop. The antipathy between them wasn't built on this revelation; it was mutual, it pre-dated this event, and it was real. There had to be something her intuition was trying to tell her.

She placed her notes on the coffee table and went to the window, drawing back the curtains to another brilliantly lit nightscape. The almost full moon reflecting on ice and snow was as awe-inspiring as the previous night. Nothing moved outside, even animals were hunkered down keeping warm, and the lake shone white between the frosted, dark trees on either shore. She couldn't bear the cold, but her soul soared whenever she was in the north in winter. Something about this landscape touched her in a way no other did. Maybe there was Viking blood in her. And why not? After all, Yorkshire had been the Viking's base when they invaded and set up home in England.

# 17

## VACATION DAY BLUES

Monday morning, the actual holiday of this long weekend, brought no police knocking on the door. For Pauline, this was a mixed blessing. It meant she wasn't in imminent danger of arrest, but it did mean another day confined almost exclusively to a small room, something she was already growing tired of. It made the thought of spending the rest of her life in prison, under even worse circumstances than these, truly frightening. She really needed to resolve this case, and quickly.

There was one ray of hope to look forward to. As he'd escorted her to her room the night before, Mike had suggested she join him for breakfast downstairs before the others came down for theirs. She looked forward to that small period of freedom.

On the other hand, when the others heard Mike's suggestion, there had been immediate outcries of dissent and a brief, unpleasant discussion at the bottom of the stairs.

"Just stay in your rooms until Pauline returns to hers," Mike had told them. "That way you can feel safe. Meanwhile, I want to discuss our plans for the day with Pauline after we've both slept on what we learned today."

"What did you learn yesterday?" Jo had asked, her usual antipathy for Pauline barely concealed.

"Not a lot," Pauline replied. "We got some background information from the Toronto police. It wasn't very illuminating. We have all lived pretty sensible lives, I'm happy to say."

"You've spent much of your life with criminals, so we're told," Tom pointed out.

"Unmasking them, yes," Pauline said calmly, refusing to be riled. "Not working with them."

"It can't help but rub off, though, can it?" Jo said.

"I'm pleased to say, it hasn't so far," Pauline replied.

"Our experience here might suggest otherwise," Saul said sarcastically.

"This murder suggests nothing of the kind, as you will know soon enough," Pauline replied.

"We heard your ski pole and your handkerchief are lying beside Arnie," Jo said. "It's like they say in the movies: an open and shut case." There was a rumble of agreement from the others at this.

The all-day drinking they'd been indulging in was making them lose their judgment, Pauline thought. However, she answered evenly, "When they say this in the movies, it's just before the detective proves it was someone else that did it and the clues were planted by the killer. How did you know about the handkerchief?"

"Everyone knows," Jo said. "Mike told us."

"I didn't," Mike said. "That piece of information we decided we wouldn't share. Anyone might have seen the ski pole if they'd looked into the room before I locked the door and went to find Pauline. But unless they stepped inside as we did, they couldn't have seen the handkerchief from just looking in the door."

"But you must have done," Jo cried. "We all know about it." She looked around at the others who nodded their agreement.

"Perhaps it's as you say," Pauline replied. "Now, if you'll excuse me, I'm going to my room."

Jo blurting out her knowledge of the handkerchief was another snippet to be added to her case notes. Was it significant? The murderer was dripping details into the group cleverly enough not to be caught out, that was for sure.

Pauline was soon seated back on her comfy couch before the fire. Away from the fires now burning in almost every room, the house was growing cold, and it felt luxurious to have this fire to herself. *Just like when I was growing up with the family huddled around the fire in the living room on winter nights.* The thought made Pauline smile. She just hoped she wouldn't be reduced to huddling around one fire here with a murderer among the group.

She heard people returning to their rooms, preparing themselves for their day of games and drinking. Her attention wasn't on the movements outside her room until she heard a high-pitched whining sound. She sprang to her feet and rushed to the door, hoping to get a clue of where the sound was coming from. The only clue was the closing of a door.

She understood now why Laurent had thought he heard wind whistling through a crack, but her own guess had been closer. It was the hinge of a door. But whose door? And how to find out when she had to have Mike escorting her everywhere?

At lunch time, Mike and Gilles escorted her down to the

kitchen where they all ate a quick meal before Mike and Pauline headed out to the garage and radio.

"Miss Riddell," Ormiston said, when she admitted to being disappointed that he had nothing new to share, "it's a public holiday for we folks in the public service and even more so for the police in the States. You must be patient. There are only so many officers and way too much police work to cover."

Pauline thanked him and reminded him she would call again in the evening. Disconsolately she returned with Mike upstairs.

"Mike," she said, as he was preparing to unlock her room door, "can we try the other doors on this floor? I'm interested in knowing if it was a squeaky door hinge that Laurent heard."

'I doubt if any of them are open, Pauline," he said. "The others wanted the keys to their rooms, and I gave them to them."

"Bother," Pauline said. "Nevertheless, I want to try."

They walked the length of the corridor, attempting to open each door. As Mike had said, they were all locked.

"It was just a thought," Pauline said, as they returned to her room. "Could you find a way to be up here whenever someone returned to their room?"

"I can try," Mike said. "It won't be easy. People will notice."

"Well, concentrate on the farther end of the corridor," Pauline said, gesturing back the way they had just come.

"Okay," Mike replied, "that's everyone but you and Jo, basically."

"Yes," Pauline said. "I'm familiar with the sound of Jo's door opening and closing and it doesn't squeak. And we know Arnie's didn't when we opened and closed it that morning, which leaves only everyone else."

Mike laughed. "That means I have to volunteer to escort all the others when they next wish to return to their rooms."

"You'll find a way," Pauline said. "Now, I'll say farewell until supper time." She stepped inside her room and closed the door.

Throughout the afternoon, Pauline heard Mike escort only two people, Bryan and Gilles, to their rooms while she listened carefully at her door. Neither of their room doors appeared to make that long drawn-out squeak but was that significant? She didn't know.

By suppertime, Pauline was thoroughly sick of her book, herself, and her room. It was a relief to leave it and join Mike and Gilles in a light supper before speaking again to Inspector Ormiston. Despite the cold, she would have happily talked to Ormiston all night, but, as he said severely, he had nothing new to share and he had a family who expected him home.

Sighing, Pauline returned with Mike to her room. It seemed her future was to be found guilty of murder and endure a lifetime in prison for she had no new ideas of her own to raise her hopes.

After the others had their evening meal, she heard them all return to their rooms. Doors were opened and closed. None of them squeaked. Pauline waited patiently at her door, listening, while they all left their rooms and went downstairs. No squeak. What did this mean? Did the door only make that sound when opened a certain way, surreptitiously, perhaps? Or had the killer learned of the noise, realized their room door was a threat and oiled the hinges?

# 18

## COFFEE NOT TEA

THE FOLLOWING MORNING, Tuesday, people in the world outside the lodge were back at work. Pauline, however, was still imprisoned and was still going over the unpleasant scenes of the days before in her mind when Mike knocked on the door and unlocked it.

"Good morning," he said when Pauline joined him in the corridor.

Pauline replied neutrally. It didn't feel like such a great morning to her. She stepped outside her room door and Mike locked the door. When she'd suggested this, she hadn't realized how distasteful this whole process would feel, she thought, gritting her teeth to avoid an unpleasant comment from escaping. With the door locked they set off along the corridor to the stairs.

"It seems our colleagues aren't as frightened of you as they like to make out," Mike said, as they reached the foot of the stairs. "They're almost all up and having breakfast."

"We should take our meal into your office then," Pauline replied. "As we talk, we may say things that upset people without our meaning to. Eavesdroppers never hear well of themselves, they say."

Mike nodded. They entered the breakfast room and those already there watched them as if expecting an attack. Pauline might have found it comical if it hadn't been so serious. Even when the case was solved and the real murderer arrested, her relationships with these people would be hard to repair. Her own resentment at their treatment of her would be hard enough to get over, never mind their embarrassment for what they had said and done. Would she be able to continue working at Neufeldt?

She took a tray, set out no doubt by Catrina for the purpose of taking Pauline's meals up to her room, and placed a plate of toast and jam on it. A small yoghurt cup and a dish of fruit salad followed. She was about to pick up the teapot and pour her usual cup of tea when she decided today, she really needed something stronger. She took the coffee jug instead.

"Wow," Jo said. "Things must be bad if you're drinking coffee."

Pauline frowned. She knew Jo watched her every move, but she hadn't fully realized the extent of it.

"I do occasionally drink coffee," Pauline said.

"I don't think so," Tom said, laughing. "In the whole time you've been with the firm, you've never drunk coffee. We've all commented on it over the past months."

Bryan walked into the room. "So, you're a tea addict too, Pauline," he said.

Feeling this was getting out of hand, Pauline did her best to keep cool in the face of these peculiarly personal comments. They weren't abusive, but again they suggested a level of scrutiny of her she'd never fully realized.

She smiled, pacifically, and said, "Does this mean you are too, Bryan?"

"Oh yes. Like you, it comes from growing up in the old country, I guess."

"Probably," Pauline replied, turning to leave the room before anyone else chimed in.

"I didn't know you grew up in Britain, Bryan," Mike said, entering the room and joining her at the breakfast counter.

"I didn't!" Bryan said, in a passable Irish accent. "I was born and spent my earliest years in Ireland, though I can't actually remember anything about it. My parents emigrated here when I was four."

Pauline laughed. "Long enough to develop a taste for tea, though."

He shook his head, grinning. "Not really, my parents drank tea all my childhood, so I did too, until I went to college. Since then, it's always been coffee except when I find someone has had a pot of tea made. Then I like to indulge in a bit of nostalgia for my lost childhood and old Ireland."

"Well, it's all yours this time," Pauline said. "I need an extra caffeine kick this morning. My brain isn't solving this new puzzle as easily as I'd like." She followed Mike out of the room and along the hallway to his office.

"Bryan's entrance lightened the mood, I thought," Mike said, as he closed his office door behind Pauline.

"It did," Pauline replied, "and I'm grateful to him. The others were casting him some dark looks though."

Mike nodded. "Waiting for us to leave, I suspect, before haranguing him. Never mind. We need to talk about today."

"Did you and Laurent speak to the police?" Pauline asked. Mike and Laurent had been set to talk to the local police before breakfast so they might learn when help may arrive.

"We did," Mike said. "The news wasn't the best. Overnight, there was fresh snow out on the highways and the plows won't start on our sideroad until later today at the earliest. The police won't be here until tomorrow, I'm sure."

"And the phones?"

"There are too many lines down," Mike said. "Repairs to our lines may be a few days yet."

"Even though we have a murdered man, a crime scene, and a murderer amongst us?" Pauline said. "Doesn't that warrant some priority?"

Mike grinned. "Inspector LaPlante, despite his French-Canadian heritage, told me in plain Anglo-Saxon that our problem was serious but so were many others in isolated homes. He suggested we never be alone during the day, and we all sleep alone with our bedroom doors locked at night."

"At least, if nothing else, he gave good advice," Pauline said.

# 19

# ANOTHER VICTIM

As Mike and Pauline were leaving the breakfast room, Bryan, reached for the teapot handle. A sharp pain in his hand made him swear and pull back. Between his middle fingers, was a puncture, caused by a fine metal sliver that was sticking out from the breadbasket right beside the teapot handle. He moved the basket away and poured tea into a mug, before turning to the others and saying, "Be careful if you want more bread. Some of the fancy metal-work on the basket has sprung loose."

As he spoke, he became aware of the angry eyes staring him.

"What?" he asked.

Jo said, affecting an unconvincing male voice, "You're a tea addict too."

"What's your point?" Bryan asked.

"That woman murdered Arnie and you're asking her if she drinks tea?" Saul said. "That's the point. We want her confined to her room, not wandering the building looking for her next victim, or sipping tea like she's done nothing wrong."

"We don't actually know she killed anyone," Bryan protested, taking his mug and a plate of bacon, sausage, scrambled eggs and toast to the table. He wrapped a napkin between his fingers, where there was still light bleeding. "I'm onboard with keeping her away from us to be safe but not branding her a murderer before there's even been a trial."

"Well, we sure didn't kill Arnie," Jo said. "Yet we're the ones that must walk around in groups until the police arrive. And lock ourselves inside our rooms at night."

"Who says so?" Bryan asked, before taking a forkful of scrambled egg to his mouth.

"The police," Saul said. "Mike spoke to them earlier on the radio. They can't get here until tomorrow at the earliest."

"It sounds like good advice," Bryan said, cutting a sausage. His tone suggested this wasn't a very interesting topic and held little interest for him.

"For you guys, maybe," Jo said. "What about me? Do you think I want you all standing outside the washroom whenever I use it?"

Bryan nodded. "True," he said. "I never thought of that." He considered for a moment, then said, "Use the one at the end of the downstairs corridor or the one in your bedroom. That way, we can be well away from the door and still know you're safe."

Jo's angry expression didn't lighten but she said nothing.

"But you do see why we don't want anyone encouraging her to wander among us freely," Saul said. "One moment's inattention and one of us could be next."

Bryan shook his head. "Her motive for killing Arnie, according to you, is pretty flimsy. She has no motive for killing anyone else, I'd say."

"We don't know that her objections to Arnie were only

what she told Mike," Tom said. "There may have been more to it."

"It still doesn't provide a motive for killing anyone else, though, does it?"

"I think Tom's point is," John said, "if we don't know the full truth about the Arnie motive, we may not know what she holds against any of us."

Tom nodded his agreement.

"Pauline joined the company not six months ago," Gilles said, bursting in on the conversation for the first time. "She didn't know any of you until then. Do any of you know of something that would lead Pauline to murder you?"

"She might see me as the only female competition for the token female spot on the Board," Jo said. "She might have something on you, Gilles, that goes back to Seaforth. She might want Tom and John gone because they're young and ambitious and she's past her prime and doesn't want to be stepped over. She might see you, Bryan, as an old man standing in her way. Who knows what madness a crazy person would regard as a motive for murder?"

Bryan put down his mug, shaking his head. "It's you who sounds a bit crazy here, Jo. She isn't in the least bit mad."

"Maybe, but I agree with Tom and John," Saul said. "We just don't know and until we do, she shouldn't be wandering around the lodge where she could be creating any sort of mischief."

There was a general nodding of heads and pointed stares at Bryan, who sat very still with a puzzled expression. They were expecting him to speak but he didn't. He remained immobile. Only his eyes darted about from one face to another.

Alarmed, Jo said, "Bryan, are you okay?"

As they waited for an answer, his eyes became still, and

the light seemed to go from them until, finally, they stared, unseeing, straight ahead. Everyone watched, puzzled, expecting Bryan to snap out of his daze. He didn't.

Gilles stepped forward and touched his shoulder. Bryan still didn't move. Gilles put his ear close to Bryan's face, hoping to hear or feel his breath. There was none. He touched Bryan's neck where a pulse should have been. Nothing.

"He's dead," Gilles said, standing upright. "Does anyone know CPR?"

It seemed no one did for there were no volunteers. "We have to try," Gilles said, attempting to push Bryan's head so his face was up. It didn't move. "He's absolutely rigid, frozen," Gilles added, giving up on his attempt.

"The teapot," John cried, in an anguished voice. "Don't anyone touch the teapot."

"Mike!" Jo said, horrified. "She's alone with Mike!" She rushed out of the room before anyone could stop her.

"I'll go with her," Saul said, hurrying out. "You all stay here." He arrived in the hall in time to see Jo pounding on the office door, shouting, "Mike. Are you okay?"

# 20

## ANOTHER CRIME SCENE INSPECTION

Pauline and Mike had barely begun their planning when there was a thump on the door that made Pauline jump. It was followed by continued pounding and Jo's voice shouting for Mike.

Mike rose and walked to the door. He opened it and said, "What?"

"She's killed another one," Jo cried, pointing at Pauline through the gap in the door.

"What are you talking about?" Pauline asked, puzzled at this new accusation.

"Bryan is dead," Jo cried. "Killed by the tea in the teapot you poisoned."

"Dead?" Mike asked, looking around at Pauline.

"He was fine when we left the room," Pauline replied. "And I certainly didn't poison any tea."

"We saw you," Jo said. "You were at the teapot, then decided on coffee. You knew Bryan drank tea, though you pretended you didn't."

"How would I know that?" Pauline asked angrily. She

knew she was letting Jo's constant accusations get to her but couldn't stop it.

"You must have seen him yesterday," Jo said. "He drank tea then."

"I saw nothing of the sort," Pauline said. "Anyway, why would I kill Bryan? I've never met him until this weekend."

"So, you say," Jo began, but Mike interjected.

"Stop it, both of you." He turned to Pauline. "We'll return to the breakfast room and see what this is about."

Bryan was sitting in a chair at the table with his back to them as they entered the room. To Pauline, he looked alive. He wasn't moving but he wasn't slumped over the table or slouching sideways, ready to fall.

She walked to his side. He was dead. There was no question. His eyes were open but drying and lifeless. She reached to touch him, and the others shouted at her to stop.

"Then tell me, is his body limp or stiff?" Pauline said.

"Stiff," Gilles said. "It's like he's frozen in place."

Pauline frowned. She knew she recognized the signs but just for the moment, the name of the poison wouldn't come to her.

"Why has he a napkin between his fingers?"

"He got jabbed by the breadbasket," Tom said, who seemed to be wavering between horror and laughter.

Pauline walked to the counter and studied the basket without touching it. As Tom had suggested, a fine sliver of metalwork had come loose and stuck out dangerously.

She turned back to the group. "Have you checked for a pulse?" she asked.

"Of course, we have," Saul said. "Do you think we're all stupid or incapable?"

"No," Pauline said, "but people often don't want to touch others without permission."

"You know he's dead," Saul said. "You killed him."

"I didn't know Bryan until we met on Friday night," Pauline replied. "How would I know to bring poison to kill him?"

"Your plan is to kill all of us," Jo said. "Bryan was just next because he drank tea."

"This is ludicrous," Pauline said.

Then Mike intervened. "No more arguments," he said. "We need to decide what to do with Bryan's body. He can't stay here like this."

"As we did with Arnie," Pauline said. "You photograph the scene from every direction. In this case, we have to move him to his room because, you're right, he can't stay here."

"I'm not eating in here again unless *you* are kept out of the room," Saul said. His statement was promptly agreed to by everyone else.

"No one can eat in the breakfast room until the police have examined the scene," Pauline said, ushering them away toward the kitchen.

"And the same goes for the kitchen too," Jo said. "We don't want you in it."

"Fine," Pauline said, as she pulled the door closed behind her. "This breakfast room door must stay closed, Mike. And to keep everyone happy, I'll take my meals in my room and stay away from the kitchen when you're all there."

"I'll escort you to your room right now," Mike said. "We'll pick up your breakfast plate on the way."

"We still need to plan today," Pauline reminded him. "Particularly questions for Inspector Ormiston."

"I think when we radio Bryan's death to the local police," Mike said, "they'll be here and taking over the investigation by lunch time, even if they have to hire a helicopter."

# 21

# MOTIVES

When Pauline and Mike were safely upstairs, the conversation in the kitchen began again in hushed voices.

"She must be mad," Saul said. "There's no other explanation."

"Mike clearly doesn't think so," Tom replied.

"I've wondered a lot about him hiring her," Jo said. "Do you think he has a relationship with her? One we don't know about, I mean?"

"I think he wanted one," Saul said. "We didn't really need her in the firm, and he was, I thought, strangely taken with her when they met last year on that government task force."

"She's too old for children," Jo said. "So marriage wouldn't be his objective."

"Maybe he just wanted companionship," John said. "He's a single man, his best days are behind him, looking at a lonely old age, maybe just a congenial companion."

Gilles laughed. "You think fifty-seven is old," he said. "That's because you're young. Mike is in the prime of his life and career."

John grinned. "Your own age isn't coloring your views there, is it, Gilles?"

"It might be," Gilles said. "But I don't think Mike is planning his decline into senility just yet nor have I heard of any relationship, existing or desired."

"Something must explain it," Saul said.

"She's good at her job and has years of experience in the field," Gilles said, "and she's worked internationally, something we're a little light on in Neufeldt. I'd say they were good enough reasons, wouldn't you?"

"I'm with Saul on this," Jo said. "I think there's more to it than we know about."

Gilles shook his head and, taking his coffee, headed out of the kitchen until he saw Mike returning to the breakfast room with his camera.

"You need a hand?" Gilles asked.

"I will once I've taken all the photos," Mike said.

Gilles followed Mike back into the kitchen where the others were still talking, their expressions mutinous.

"It's best you all decamp to another room," Mike said. "I'll take the pictures and Gilles and I will carry Bryan upstairs."

As they filed out, Mike entered the breakfast room, set up his tripod and adjusted the camera settings for the light. He placed a sheet of paper with a list of poses on the table. Turning to Gilles, who'd followed him in after shepherding the others away, Mike said, "Pauline says we need all these views. Can you check them off as I take them, please?"

They worked steadily, taking wide shots of the scene and close-up shots of the body, cup, plate, table, chair, breadbasket, and teapot. Mike changed the film and began again.

"I'm doing it twice on two separate rolls of film with slightly different settings in case something's wrong with the first," he explained. "I'm a good photographer but I've never had to take photos that are this important; I'm nervous I'll get it wrong."

"I assume, as you're using Pauline's list of shots, you don't think she's the murderer?" Gilles said.

"You're right, I don't," Mike said, not pausing his shooting to speak. "It's possible, of course, but then I might be the murderer, or you might be. One of the people here certainly is. I'm using Pauline's list because, murderer or not, she has experience in this kind of thing, and I don't."

Gilles nodded. "Have you any ideas?"

"My head is full of ideas and none of them have any evidence or even rationale behind them."

"That's what I think too," Gilles said. "I look at each one of us and try to imagine some scenario where this could be the outcome and I don't see it at all."

"Pauline says it has to be something outside our normal interactions because the two victims, Arnie and Bryan, have no connection to each other through work," Mike said, winding on the film and removing it from the camera.

"We don't know enough about our colleagues outside work to solve it from here," Gilles said.

"That's where Pauline's connections to the police help," Mike said, laying the camera on the countertop and sizing up the body.

"Do you have anything that would make carrying him easier, more dignified?" Gilles asked.

"I'll ask Catrina for some sheets or blankets. That way we can lay him out on them and if Laurent helps by supporting the middle, we can get him upstairs to his room."

Gilles took hold of Bryan's arm. "He's still as stiff as a board. I thought it took time for rigor mortis to set in."

"Pauline says it isn't rigor. She says it's an alkaloid poison that paralyses and kills. It's what South American natives use for hunting."

"Nobody here is South American and nor have they been there recently," Gilles said. "They would have mentioned a trip like that."

"Apparently, it's also used in hospitals but in smaller doses."

"Nobody has mentioned being in hospital recently," Gilles said, his face creased in thought.

"Someone may volunteer at a local hospital and not mentioned it," Mike said, heading out to find Catrina and Laurent. "You know the sort of thing. Doing good by stealth, only to be discovered doing it when the time is right."

Gilles shook his head, but Mike was gone. He muttered, "If that's how they got it, they've been planning this a long time. And why kill Arnie with a ski pole when they had this stuff available?" He paused, then added, quietly, "I hope they don't have any more."

From the lounge, Jo, Saul, Tom, and John watched Mike, Gilles, and Laurent carry the awkwardly shaped body upstairs.

"I wish they still hanged people," Saul said. "I liked old Bryan and hate what has happened to him."

"It's rotten," Jo agreed. "Being humiliated by the company and then killed by a maniac. What a way to end your life."

"Nobody mentioned him being humiliated by the firm?" Tom said.

Saul stepped in before Jo could speak. "I think Jo may have that the wrong way round," he said. "They chose Mike for the CEO position ahead of Bryan, who had more seniority, but I think they gave Bryan the option of a good package. He chose to stay on in an advisory capacity."

Jo snorted. "Bryan only says that to cope with his pain. Truth is, they left him swinging in the breeze for all the world to see. Whatever he'd done wrong, they made sure he paid for it."

"Then it's even more strange that anyone should want to kill Bryan," John said. "What possible motive could anyone have?"

"None," Saul said. "That's why it has to be a mad person who killed once with Arnie and then found they couldn't stop."

John nodded. "I guess so. I'm just glad I'm too new here to be on her radar."

"My guess is at this point there's no reason at all why she's killing us," Jo said. "You're as likely to be next as any of us. I never liked her. I knew there was something behind that cold, too-calm exterior."

"Maybe it's been her time working with criminals," Tom said. "Somebody said that, I seem to remember."

"That and a lonely, solitary life," Jo said. "I'd feel sorry for her if I didn't fear for my life. She's never liked me."

"Like Mike said, the police will arrive soon, now they know there's a second murder," Saul said. "So long as she isn't allowed out without a chaperone, we'll be okay. In a way, this second murder, so obviously done by her, has made it easier for us to keep safe."

"True," Tom said. "Until Bryan's death, I was on the fence when it came to who killed Arnie. Now, there's no doubt, and I'll run if I even see her approaching."

John grinned and said, "I'm with you, buddy."

Jo laughed. "Then it was lucky I wasn't looking for you young men to save me."

"Nah," John said, "We were looking for you to save us. Seriously, though, how are we going to be sure of anything now? Bryan drank the tea after Miss Murderer had tampered with it. We were just lucky we'd all eaten before she arrived. How do we know anything is safe? Did she go in the kitchen?"

"I hadn't thought of that," Saul said, his expression one of dismay. "I did eat a Danish after she'd been there."

"You're still alive," Jo said. "So, the Danish are safe."

"We should warn the Pomerleaus," Saul said.

"No need, Mike told them to leave everything in the breakfast room as it was until the police arrive," Tom said.

"We should have left Bryan too," Jo said, frowning. "We should have stopped Mike and Gilles. What they've done is tampering with evidence." She paused and then added, grimly, "But maybe that's what they intended. They're both her friends."

They were silent as they worked through this latest thought. Then they heard Mike and Pauline coming back down the stairs and they moved to the entranceway to watch them go by.

"Why is she going to talk to the police?" Jo demanded of Mike, as he passed by.

"Because Pauline knows Inspector Ormiston and he will provide information to her and not to me, or you," Mike responded without stopping.

"I don't like it," Saul said. "That woman is the most likely murderer and she's the one who is managing the information between us and the police."

Tom nodded. "She could frame any one of us for the murders with a few well-placed words."

"I don't see how," Saul said.

"I do," Jo said. "She could say I slept with Arnie and

killed him for something he did to me, and I then accidentally killed Bryan when I was trying to kill her. You killed Arnie because of something that happened in the past and killed Bryan accidentally in the same way I might have done. You get the picture?"

"I'm glad you didn't include Tom and me in that," John said, grinning. "It sometimes pays to be the newbie on the block."

"She's sly," Jo said. "Who knows what she could suggest against you two."

"My mom bumped into her shopping trolley in the A&P," Tom suggested, grinning.

"You can jeer, if you want," Jo said, savagely. "She has experience that could help her frame any of us. We're amateurs here. She's the professional."

"I've just had a thought," John said. "Could she be killing a lot of people *without* a motive to hide the one murder *with* a motive?"

There was a moment of silence while the others digested this idea. Eventually, Saul said, slowly, "You may have something there. We've all assumed Arnie was the target but what if he was just expedient? What if she heard Jo leave Arnie's room, took advantage of the moment to slip in while Arnie was asleep or befuddled, and killed him?"

"And killed Bryan because he too was expedient?" Jo said. "I think you're right, John. These two killings are motiveless, and the real victim is one of us."

"Should we warn Mike?" Tom asked. "After all, he's the one most likely to be the real target."

"It could be Gilles," John said. "After all, he's known her longer than any of us. Maybe it's something in their shared past that she's seeking revenge for."

"The point is," Saul said, "if John is right, it could be any of us. We all need to search our memories from the time she arrived to see where a motive might lie."

Tom shrugged. "Again, I haven't had one disagreement with her so I'm in the clear."

"You're not thinking deep enough," Jo said. "It isn't something that *you* were okay with, it's something you didn't realize she *wasn't* okay with."

"It may not even be something you said or did," Saul added. "It could be something you were given that she thought should have come to her."

"We'll go mad if we spend hours on minor matters," Tom protested. "It must be something big for murder to happen."

"I wouldn't bank on it," Jo said. "People are murdered over trifles."

"Among gangsters and street hoodlums maybe, not in our world," Tom said, firmly closing a discussion that was beginning to unnerve him.

# 22

## DID THE BUTLER DO IT?

As THEY ENTERED the garage for their morning call to Ormiston, Mike took up the conversation that they'd stopped while passing the others gathered in the lobby. They'd been talking about the evidence, why the others were so sure Pauline was guilty and why they were growing concerned about Pauline talking to the police. "When they consider the evidence and then they see you talking to the police with them excluded, you must agree their point is a fair one, Pauline."

Pauline frowned. "Maybe, but Jo's casting aspersions my way is very foolish. The police will look at her more closely because of it."

She opened the truck door and climbed onto the driver seat before unclipping the radio handset from the dashboard. It took a minute or so before she was speaking to Inspector Ormiston.

"Good morning, Miss Riddell. To what do I owe this early call?"

"There's been another murder," Pauline said.

"Who?"

"Bryan O'Connell," Pauline replied. "He was poisoned. Do you have anything new to relate about him?"

"Nothing criminal," Ormiston said. "His private life was colorful in his younger days, but no one cares much about that sort of thing now. Have you told Inspector LaPlante?"

"Not yet," Pauline replied. "I was hoping you'd have something that would shed light on this unpleasantness."

"We have nothing new on the others and we're struggling to find much of anything about John Beresford. The police down south have nothing against him. What they know is, his mother was a single mother. She and John moved to Knoxville about six years ago when she became librarian in the local library. They didn't know anyone there. They haven't found any record of who John's father is."

"You found nothing new about Saul, Tom, or Gilles?"

"Nothing beyond the usual dates of birth and so on," Ormiston said. "We had all the dirt on them right away. No, they're a suspiciously clean bunch of folks, I'd say."

"And the Pomerleaus?"

"Ah, now there might be something there, though how it relates to the two victims I couldn't say," Ormiston said.

"Well?"

"They were both arrested in Toronto nearly twenty years ago when they were at college here. They were on a protest at a logging company's head office that turned nasty. They were both charged with assault though never convicted."

"Not a very serious assault then," Pauline said.

"They pleaded guilty to lesser charges and were fined," Ormiston said. "The usual Sixties demo stuff; everyone – police and protesters – letting off steam on an otherwise boring weekend, basically."

"You're a cynic, Inspector," Pauline said. "I'm sure deep feelings were being felt by all."

"Possibly," Ormiston replied. "However, it does suggest they might commit violence if they believed they had cause."

"It was twenty years ago and minor," Pauline mused.

"True but suggestive, is all I'm saying. What was the poison by the way? Do you know?"

"I think curarine but I'm not an expert," Pauline said. "If it is, it could only have come from a hospital or a drug store. Someone may have reported it missing."

"We'll check into it," Ormiston said.

"If there's nothing else, Inspector," Pauline said, "I'm going to contact Inspector LaPlante."

"Do that and get him out there to help, Miss Riddell, before you're killed too."

It took some time to get Inspector LaPlante to the radio but when he heard of the second death, he assured them he'd fly in around lunchtime with a forensic team.

"That's good news, Inspector," Pauline said. "Have you received the background on everyone here from Inspector Ormiston?"

"I have. I'll bring them with me. By the way, Miss Riddell, Inspector Ormiston speaks highly of you, but he also says you are under suspicion for these murders. Is that true?"

Pauline glanced at Mike who was listening impatiently before saying, "It's true, Inspector. I'll hand you over to Mike Armitage who is the head of Neufeldt, the firm I'm a partner in, and my host here. He can explain more neutrally than I will." She handed the microphone to Mike and slid out of the truck cabin.

Mike took her place and explained how the group had come to believe Pauline was the murderer.

"You clearly don't share their opinion," LaPlante said.

"I don't, and I think I can say she doesn't believe I'm the murderer either," Mike said, glancing at Pauline.

"She certainly didn't ask for your background," LaPlante said, with a short laugh.

"We have a question for you," Mike said. "Inspector Ormiston gave us history but have you any recent details on the Pomerleaus?"

"My people are looking into that now, but I certainly don't remember anything."

"It's much more likely it's one of the Toronto group," Mike said.

"Both victims are from that group," LaPlante said, "so I agree with your assessment. Nevertheless, we'll follow up on the Pomerleaus."

Pauline chimed in, reminding him of his promise. "We need you here as soon as possible, Inspector."

"I won't be any longer than I need to be," he said. "I'm assembling a team and awaiting background details. The helicopter is on its way here so the moment it arrives, we'll be on our way to you."

After signing off, Pauline and Mike returned to the house. "Their arrival may bring an end to the murders," Mike said.

"I hope so, but I think the second murder was a mistake," Pauline responded. "I think the poison was meant for me, but I chose coffee. Bryan drank it instead."

Mike frowned. "And you think the murderer might try again before the police arrive?"

"I think they might," Pauline said. "I'll continue blocking my room door with furniture when I'm inside and I won't eat or drink anything until the police are here."

They crossed the lobby under the accusing eyes of the

other guests. Mike paused to tell them the police would soon be on their way.

"Good," Jo said. "Then they'll take her away and we can all feel safe again."

"The police will follow the evidence," Pauline responded sharply.

"As all the evidence points in your direction," Saul said, "that's basically what Jo said."

Pauline shook her head and headed upstairs, followed by Mike. Once she was safely inside her room, she once again turned her attention to the problem of who killed Arnie and Bryan. Sadly, though she paced the floor from wall to wall, she still had too little data to formulate a reasonable theory.

# 23

## SEEKING RE-ASSURANCE

"When exactly will they be here?" John asked when Mike re-joined them

"Soon," he said. "They're just waiting for the chopper to arrive."

"Then they can take us out with them when they go," Saul said.

"I don't think it will be that kind of helicopter," Mike replied. "And I don't think they run a passenger service."

"We want to leave," Tom said. "All of us."

"The police will probably need all day to take statements and do forensics so nobody will be able to leave until at least tomorrow, I imagine."

"Did they say if the snowplows are on their way?" Gilles asked.

"No," Mike said. "I didn't ask."

Gilles nodded. "They'll know though and we can ask them when they arrive."

"I guess so," Mike replied. "Meanwhile, we need to keep together so no one can become another victim."

"Huh," Jo said, "the murderer is alone upstairs, and we only have your word she's locked in."

There was a rumble of agreement so Mike said, "If it will set your minds at rest, we can all go up to the door where you can try and open it. That way, you'll know."

They quickly climbed the stairs, and each tried the door handle of Pauline's room.

"Hey," Jo said, as she tried the handle, the last one to do so, "how do we know she's even in this room?" She hammered on the door. "Are you there?" she yelled.

"I'm here."

Jo stared at the door as though considering whether Pauline's voice really had come from the other side. Deciding it must, she turned to Mike and asked, "And you have the key?"

Mike produced the old-fashioned iron key from his pocket, placed in the lock, and turned it. He opened the door as far as it would go, which was barely an inch, then closed and locked it again.

"Happy now?" he asked.

The group had the grace to look embarrassed. But they nodded, turned, and headed back downstairs.

"Sorry for that, Pauline," Mike said, loudly enough to be heard by Pauline and the retreating group. "They needed re-assurance."

"I wouldn't mind some of that too," Pauline replied. "You do still have that key?"

"I do. I replaced it in my pocket and there it will stay until the police arrive."

"Then we wait and think," Pauline said, "unless they aren't here by one o'clock, in which case I want to radio Inspector Ormiston again."

"He hadn't much to share this morning," Mike reminded her.

"Maybe not, but information gathering is slow and goes in fits and starts. If there's something new, I want to know it as soon as I can because we haven't gotten the facts we need to solve this case. Something is missing."

# 24

## LIKE CAMPING AS A KID

Mike returned to the games room where the rest of his guests were in furious discussion about their predicament.

"She's locked in," Tom was saying as Mike arrived. He stopped to see if Mike had anything new to impart.

"It may interest you to know," Mike said, "that Pauline has barred the door to her room from the inside." He paused, before continuing, "You may think she's the killer, but she believes the killer is out here and means to kill *her*."

"Just a pantomime to convince you of her innocence," Saul said. "It doesn't convince me."

"Nor me," Jo said. "In fact, quite the reverse. I think she's trying to fool us into letting her out."

"There's no time left for us to be convinced," Mike said. "The police will be here before you could all change your mind."

"How are we going to eat in safety if the police can't get here?" John asked.

Mike laughed. "Only a young man would think about eating at a time like this."

John grinned sheepishly. "Well, I hadn't had my breakfast before Bryan died and I'm hungry."

"We'll all watch Catrina in the kitchen as she prepares lunch," Mike suggested. "That way we can see pantry to plate. Would that satisfy you?"

"Only if we all ate the same and I watched everyone eat before me," Jo said.

"Me too," Saul agreed.

"The pantry has cans of soup, beans, and meat," Mike said. "Take one, open it yourself, cook it and eat it. How's that?"

"Works for me," John replied, brightening. "In fact, I'm going to do that right now, if you don't mind?"

"Go right ahead," Mike said.

John was about to leave when Jo cried, "Hey! No one goes anywhere alone, remember?"

"Sorry, forgot," John said. "Who'll come with me?"

"I will," Gilles said. "I wouldn't mind a snack myself."

"Me too," Tom said.

"Then we should all go," Mike said. "And remember also, no one enters the breakfast room."

"I'm happy here," Jo said.

Saul nodded. "I'll stay with Jo."

"I'm going to make coffee in the kitchen," Mike added, "if Catrina isn't there to make it for us. Do you two want some?"

"No!" Jo said. "Sorry, Mike. I'm not eating or drinking anything I don't watch the preparation of from beginning to end."

Mike nodded and signaled Gilles, John, and Tom to leave for the kitchen.

When they were gone, Jo said quietly, "It couldn't be Mike, could it?"

"Nah, I think he was just being polite when he offered to bring you a coffee. He forgot the circumstances," Saul replied.

Jo frowned. "He's been in the business a long time and must have known Arnie for years. Why did he invite him this weekend? And Bryan might have been a thorn in Mike's side; we only have his word he found Bryan helpful."

"I see what you mean," Saul replied thoughtfully. "Is there something going down at work that Arnie and Bryan might have recognized, and their knowing could have become a problem?"

"I'm not in the Board's confidence," Jo said, bitterly.

"Me neither," Saul said. "Only Bryan would know and he's now dead."

"Exactly my point," Jo replied. "Gilles might. He's old enough to be in the 'boys club' that runs Neufeldt."

"He's too new, I think," Saul said. "It wouldn't hurt to ask, though, would it?"

"The first of us that gets him far enough away from the others for safety, asks him."

"Agreed," Saul said, "We'll have to be really careful because if it is Mike, and he gets wind of it, we'll be next."

"And our questions can't be too obvious because there might be others nearby," Jo said, thoughtfully. "Just something that sounds harmless, something like, 'what's next in the future for Neufeldt' maybe."

Saul nodded. "When they return, after a short interval maybe we say we want to make coffee and angle to have Gilles accompany us."

"You know," Jo said slowly, "thinking like this makes me wonder if our Miss Riddell may not be right after all. The killer is out here. It isn't a comfortable feeling."

"What about Gilles?" Saul said. "He's been in the business as long as Mike and he too might have felt Arnie's arrival, and Bryan's presence, were obstacles to where he wanted to be. Maybe he has something driving him to want the top spot here. Maybe Mike is next?"

"They could be in it together and framing Pauline because she's known to dabble in crime," Jo mused. She shook her head. "When you stop and think, you see all sorts of possibilities. I may follow Pauline's example and lock myself in my room."

Saul laughed. "If we stay together, we're safe."

"Hah! We were all there when Bryan died. It didn't save him."

"If this was a movie," Saul said, "it would be exciting – but it's not."

Jo nodded. "I hear them returning. We need to be ready for the opportunity to arise."

John and Tom led the way into the room, each carrying an opened can of beans, a spoon and a mug of coffee.

"We decided not to risk the crockery," John laughed, as he took a seat next to Jo. "Straight from the can, like going camping as a kid."

"Have you even warmed them?" Jo asked, with a disapproving expression.

"No," John said, scooping out a heaping mouthful of beans. "They're just as good cold." He put the beans in his mouth and chewed slowly, wearing a happy smile.

"Ugh," Jo said, shaking her head.

"The coffee smells good though," Saul said.

"There's still some in the pot," Tom replied. "If you want it."

"After I've seen you folks drink and survive," Saul said, grinning.

"Not even then," Jo snapped. "Who's to say the last person out of the kitchen didn't spike the coffee pot?"

Gilles laughed. "I was last out and I didn't."

"Or someone could be in there now, spiking it," Saul said.

"Then make your own coffee," Mike said.

"I intend to," Saul said, rising from his chair. "Like to show me how that coffee machine works, Gilles? It has more buttons than the Starship Enterprise. You'd better come too, if you want a cup, Jo."

Gilles sighed. "You couldn't have come with us all before?"

"I didn't know I wanted one until you folks arrived back. The smell of fresh coffee was too much."

"I can show them, if you like, Gilles," Mike said.

Gilles shook his head. "I'll go. I need the exercise anyhow."

# 25

## MORE ICE COMING

WHEN THE THREE had left the room, Tom said, "Those two are just plain contrary."

Mike nodded. "Seems like it," he said. "It's been eye-opening watching what has happened here over the past two days." He lapsed into silence without further explanation.

"I hope you don't think I'm pointing fingers, Mike," Tom added, cautiously.

"Not at all," Mike said. "I know exactly what you mean. We're all on edge, I guess, and it affects us all differently."

"You don't seem to be convinced by the evidence that points to Pauline," John said. "I don't know her so I'm keeping an open mind, but it does seem to be clear. At least Jo and Saul think so."

"Pauline has solved mysteries all over the world, as well as in her day job of seeking out financial irregularities," Mike said. "If she murdered someone, there wouldn't be *any* clues left to find. It would be a very strange strategy to leave clues hoping that would convince us it wasn't her."

John nodded. "I hadn't thought of that but then, I didn't know she'd solved murders before."

"Lots," Mike said. "In England and Australia, as well as here in Canada." He was about to continue when Laurent Pomerleau called to him from the kitchen door.

"What is it?" Mike asked, rising to his feet.

"The police are on the radio. They want to speak to you."

Mike hurried off, following Laurent out into the garage.

"Which police, Laurent?" he asked.

"Local ones," Laurent said.

Mike picked up the microphone, pressed the button and said, "Is that you, Inspector?"

"It is," LaPlante replied. "The latest weather forecast is calling for another ice storm, a fast moving one arriving this afternoon and evening. That means the chopper is grounded until it's over. We won't be joining you now until tomorrow."

Mike groaned. "There's no way you can get here by road or snowmobile?"

"They haven't even begun plowing the road to your place and our rules are strict about what we can and can't do in ice storms. Tomorrow first thing, provided the storm doesn't linger."

"My guests are extremely anxious," Mike replied, "as I'm sure you can imagine."

"Take the precautions we've talked about and that should keep everyone safe."

"We thought so too, until Bryan died right in front of our eyes this morning," Mike said.

"I do understand," LaPlante replied, "but my hands are tied. You must keep everyone in sight of each other. And keep individuals away from the food."

"Easier said than done, Inspector," Mike replied sharply.

"No one will eat anything they haven't seen taken from a closed package and heated in their presence. It's that tense."

"You're all adults. Talk it through until you have a system that works. Failing everything, those who won't eat can wait until we arrive in the morning. They won't take any hurt. Now, I must go."

Mike switched off the radio and hung the mouthpiece on the set. "Any suggestions about the meals, Laurent?"

"Best ask Catrina," Laurent replied, with a grin. "No one would want me cooking even if there wasn't a poisoner around."

Once back in the warmth of the kitchen, however, Catrina declined any intention of cooking any more meals. In her mind, too many of the comments after Bryan's death had seemed very pointed.

"I'm sure no one thought anything of the sort," Mike said, confidently.

"No matter," Catrina replied. "It's best they cook for themselves, then they'll be happy."

"Do we have enough canned or dried goods for everyone to eat that way?" Mike asked.

Catrina shook her head. "Only the emergency stocks. Everything I got in for this weekend was fresh."

"Well, I, and anyone else who wants to, can eat the fresh stuff and that will leave more of the sealed foods for those who are too nervous."

"Okay," Catrina replied, "I'll put the emergency rations on the countertop, the fresh is in the fridge. Thank heavens for the generator, though Laurent says fuel is running low, by the way. I'll clean up after everyone is finished."

"Thanks, Catrina," Mike said. "I'm sorry for all this."

"Not your fault," Catrina said. She smiled and added, "unless it *is* your fault, of course."

Mike laughed. "It isn't but there could soon be a murder that might be. Anyhow, I'll go and tell the others. They'll be delighted."

The others, however, were not delighted – and said so, loudly.

Mike explained about the eating arrangements and finished by saying, "Now I'll go tell Pauline the good news."

"Not on your own, you won't," Jo said, belligerently. She seemed the most put out over this delay. "Always two of us, remember?"

"I'm happy to have any one of you chaperone me," Mike said.

"We'll go," Jo said, glancing at Saul who nodded agreement.

"Don't leave your coffee behind," Mike teased them, as they rose to their feet.

They grabbed their coffee mugs and followed Mike upstairs to Pauline's bedroom door. Mike knocked and said, "Pauline, it's me."

They heard Pauline approaching the door from the other side. "Yes?"

"There's another storm coming, and the police won't be here until tomorrow morning."

"I thought there might be," Pauline replied. "I've been watching from the window and the sky has been darkening this past hour."

"We'll repeat yesterday's procedure where I collect you and bring you downstairs at lunch time." He explained the changed cooking arrangements.

"Then make it around twelve-thirty and we'll radio Inspector Ormiston at one, as usual."

"Very well," Mike said. "He didn't have much new to tell us last night, though."

"There has to be something," Pauline said, "and provided they don't stop looking, they should find it."

Jo and Saul watched and listened with great suspicion, as if trying to decipher a code. Then Jo asked, "Why do you say something's missing?"

"Because no one here has a real motive on the face of it," Pauline replied. "Unless the murderer is simply mad, and I don't think that's the case."

"I can think of motives," Jo said.

Pauline's sigh was audible even through the door. "We can all think of motives," she said. "But I haven't thought of one strong enough to warrant one death, let alone two. Have you?"

Jo flushed angrily. She seemed about to explode but then appeared to change her mind. With an effort, she said, "Well, no, I guess not."

"We'll leave you to your thoughts, Pauline," Mike said. "I'll be back around twelve-thirty."

As the three walked away, Jo said, "Now I'm even more sure it's her. If all the motives I can think of could lead to murder, why then can't the great detective think of them?"

# 26

## IT'S GETTING SERIOUS

AT LUNCH TIME, however, Inspector Ormiston couldn't add much new information, except to say, "John Beresford wasn't born in the States, so the police down there tell me."

Pauline turned to Mike, "Has he mentioned to you his place of birth?"

Mike shook his head. His expression wryly amused. "No and I never asked, any more than I asked yours or anyone I've hired. If he joins us, we'll have it and his birthdate for tax purposes but that's about it."

"Could he be Canadian?" she asked.

"He says he's an American," Mike replied.

"That's just citizenship," Pauline said. "I'm a Canadian citizen but I'm English, or British, if you like."

"Again, all I can say is, if he was hired, he would have to provide the right identification for us to manage his salary and tax obligations, but he isn't hired so I can't. Maybe he was born in England, too."

Pauline shook her head. "Only if he left before he began speaking," she said. "There's not a trace of it in his accent. It's North American and, on the face of it, American."

"Then he probably is," Mike said.

"I don't think so," Pauline said. "He sounds like someone putting on an act. Underneath it, I hear an Ontario accent."

Mike laughed. "You're an expert in accents too, Pauline?"

Pauline smiled. "I'm British," she said. "We're born with an ear for accent. From childhood we can tell where someone is from just by hearing them speak."

"Does it work over here though?" Mike asked.

"Not as well," Pauline admitted, "or I may be just too new. I still think I'm right about John." She turned her attention back to the radio. "Inspector, can you find out where he was born?"

"It will take time, but if it was here in Ontario we'll find it," Ormiston said. "If he left as a child, what value is it to know that?"

"I don't know," Pauline said. "He's just the unknown one. None of the others have mysterious pasts."

Deep in thought, Pauline returned to her room, under the watchful gaze of her fellow guests. Had she ever met a John Beresford at any time in her career? He would have been a child or teenager if she had. And why would he hate Arnie enough to kill him? By the time she'd reached her room, entered it, and had the door locked behind her, she'd decided this was likely another dead end.

She pushed the small dresser she was using as a barricade across the door. She now had another day where her hidden enemy was waiting his or her opportunity to finish what they'd started. She crossed the floor to the closet where her suitcase was stored, opened it and removed the small Beretta she'd bought years before. She'd bought it because it was the gun that had been James Bond's favorite gun, before M made him replace it with a newer, heavier one. She knew this from the books, which she approved of for their patriotic flavor though she didn't much care for. Mr. Bond's behavior left much to be desired, in her mind. In fact, she'd bought it because the Secret Service armorer had told Bond that the Beretta was a lady's gun. Trying it out in the shop, Pauline had understood what he meant. The gun's size fitted a woman's hand perfectly.

Sitting on the bed, she removed the clip and checked the action, running through the inspections her instructor had shown her all those years ago. She'd never had to use it, but it was re-assuring to know it was there. Her checks complete, she placed it in her jacket pocket and walked to the window where the first drops of icy rain were hitting the glass with sharp smacks. More long, wakeful hours lay ahead and, as these lonely vigils often did, it reminded her of Newcastle, 1953, and Inspector Ramsay. Her heart skipped a beat. She sighed. Ramsay was more than a mentor in her mind. Like her dead fiancé, Stephen, he held a special place of great affection in her heart that time and distance could not erase.

## 27

# ESCAPES PLANNED

"WHAT DID the police actually say, Mike?" Jo demanded, when the group was once again downstairs and away from Pauline's hearing. "And why can't we listen in on these conversations?"

"I told you," Mike said. "Provided the storm ends as forecast, they will be here tomorrow morning. As to listening in, it's out of the question. The only reason the police give us any information at all is because Pauline has their confidence, as I've also told you before."

"It's not good enough," Saul said. "They can still talk to her if they want but we should know if there's anything being said about us."

"I'm telling you all I can," Mike said. "They won't tell us anything if everyone is listening in."

"Then they *shouldn't* be telling anyone anything," Saul said. "The most likely person to be the murderer is the one who is being armed with information to frame us. No more calls. That's what I say." He turned to the others, "Well?"

"I agree," Jo replied.

Tom paused; his indecision clearly etched on his face.

"I'd like this mystery solved quickly, as we all do, but I can't help but think Saul is right. One of the suspects, and we're all suspects, is being given information that the rest of us aren't and it makes me nervous."

"I have to agree with Tom," John said. "It's unfair."

Mike looked to Gilles, who grinned. "Pauline can have my whole life story from them or me," he said. "I've nothing to hide."

"That's not the issue, Gilles," Jo cried. "What's happening is just plain wrong. She really could be the murderer."

Gilles shook his head. "Of everyone here, Pauline is the one least likely to kill anyone." He raised his hand to stem the chorus of objection he could see growing. "I understand why you feel the way you do but I don't buy it."

Mike put an end to the growing tumult by saying, "Pauline has the trust of the police and that's good enough for me. It's my house, my decision."

There was silence but the sullen expressions of Jo and Saul spoke plainly of their disapproval.

"Mike's right, you know," John said. "We need to keep ourselves busy and stop brooding on this mess. What about another pool tournament?"

"I'm good with that," Tom said, looking at the others who showed no sign of joining in.

"It's just the two of us then," John said. "Let's go."

They headed to the games room, leaving the others frozen in sullen silence.

"Mike," Gilles said, "I know we said no business this weekend, but I think things have moved on from there. Can I talk to you for a few minutes about the Renseiller audit I'm doing?"

Mike nodded and he and Gilles left Jo and Saul in possession of the lounge area.

"I don't like the way the group splits up into these factions," Saul said, when he was sure they were alone. "The two kids, the two remaining old guys, and us singled out."

Jo nodded. "I know what you mean. This could hurt us when it's all over."

"You think Mike will hold a grudge, knowing we were right, and he was disastrously wrong?"

"Exactly," Jo replied. "Bosses don't like to be shown up by their underlings. For years to come, maybe forever, every time he sees one of us, our good judgment will be a constant reminder to him of his bad judgment."

"What a mess," Saul said. "Looking for a new place in our small industry isn't easy. Everyone knows what everyone is doing. And Mike will poison any chance we might have at a different firm."

Jo nodded. "I've been thinking of starting my own business anyhow. Ever since he brought in that woman over my head."

"She isn't your boss," Saul reminded her.

"No but she is the token female they'll put on the board," Jo said. "That should have been my spot and no, I don't care that it would have been an affirmative action hire. I would have done a great job and they'd soon have forgotten how I got there."

Saul didn't answer right away. His brow was creased in thought. After a minute, he said, "Could you take many of your clients with you, to your own business?"

"I've been sounding them out. I think two for sure, maybe four. Enough to begin, anyhow."

"I think I could bring similar numbers," Saul said. "We could pool our clients in a joint venture."

It was Jo's turn to consider. After a moment, she replied, "Okay, here's what I suggest. If we get out of here alive, we sound out our clients, get commitments from them, and decide by the end of March. Agreed?"

"Agreed," Saul said. He grinned, adding, "What we do until we get out of here is the more pressing problem right now."

"Mike has a well-appointed gym at the back of the house. It's away from the others and we can see anyone approaching, which means we can't be surprised. Are you up for some gym time?"

Saul nodded. "Why not. We'll have to be fit to run our own business because at the beginning, we won't have staff."

"I'm going to change into something more athletic," Jo said, standing abruptly. A sudden onslaught of ice battering the window caught her attention. She shivered. "The cops were right not to travel."

Saul, watching the wintry blast splashing a thickening coat of ice on the glass, agreed.

UPSTAIRS, Pauline's attention had also been caught by the increasing severity of the storm and she too watched the ice growing on her bedroom window, obliterating the view. If this didn't die down soon, the police wouldn't even arrive tomorrow, which meant she might have yet another day locked up. She was in a beautiful room with everything she could want, and it was intolerable – how much worse it would be for her in a prison cell.

She returned to her seat beside the wood fire, and to the notes she'd made from Ormiston's information. All this background was creating a growing list of possible explanations. Some of which were becoming wildly fanciful. Was there a loft and could a madman or woman be hiding in it, like Mrs. Rochester in *Jane Eyre*? Pauline smiled. Too much sherry yesterday evening was the source of that theory.

She'd barely settled herself when she heard footsteps ascending the stairs. Pauline recognized the voices approaching, Jo and Saul, the two who she most feared might try to do her harm. From the moment she'd arrived at Neufeldt, she'd sensed their antipathy; this weekend it had gone into full-blown paranoia. She reached to the cushion on the small couch where she was sitting and grasped the Beretta's handle.

The voices passed by her door without stopping and she released the gun. Their room doors opened and closed. Still no squeaky hinge.

Jo and Saul's voices had been low, but she'd heard enough to know they were changing for the gym. Her mind quickly considered the ways gym equipment could be made to 'accidentally' kill someone and smiled. She wondered if either of them had considered that possibility or were they too sure of the other's innocence?

Jo and Saul (*why do I always think of them in that order?*) spent only a few minutes changing and she heard them again out in the corridor. They paused outside her bedroom door and Pauline reached for her gun again. She surmised they were probably just listening at the door, hoping to hear something they could use against her. The silence lasted only a minute before she heard them move on. She relaxed but this brief interlude made it seem a long time to wait until the next meal and her radio call to Ormiston and LaPlante.

# 28

## STILL NO GOOD MOTIVE

THE OTHERS HAD all eaten before Pauline was escorted by Mike down to the kitchen for lunch. As always, when she was allowed out, they stared at her, muttering darkly in stage whispers they knew she could hear.

"There she goes," Pauline heard Saul say, "off to poison the police's investigation with misinformation about us."

"Not me," Tom replied. "Like I said, it would have to be something my mom did to her."

"Tom's right, Saul. You, Jo, Gilles and Mike, are the only ones she can finger," John said. "Us new kids on the block are off the hook."

"Maybe your mom bumped her shopping trolley in the supermarket too, John," Tom said, laughing. "That's all she can have on me 'cos I didn't know either Arnie or Bryan."

"Same here," John said, "though I did hear Arnie got someone killed."

"Where did you hear that?" Gilles asked, sharply.

John hesitated. "I don't know. I just heard it. Why? Isn't it true?"

"Unlikely," Jo said, with a harsh laugh, "but that's the sort of thing that could be a motive."

"Arnie was an auditor, not a gangster," Gilles said. "Throwing out wild accusations like that isn't going to help."

"You can see how rattled everyone is," Mike said to Pauline when they had walked out of the others' hearing. "Haven't you any ideas?"

"I've lots of ideas but until I get more information, I can't decide which is right and which is just a guess," Pauline said. "By the way, there isn't a loft or basement to the lodge, is there? Somewhere someone could be hiding out?"

"Nothing except the outbuildings where the boats and vehicles are kept," Mike said. "And the Pomerleaus are living above the garage so it's unlikely anyone is hiding there. Anyhow, those buildings aren't heated. No one could have survived the last two nights without heat."

"I didn't think there were," Pauline said. "But I thought it best to be sure."

"I had thought of it and checked the outbuildings right after Arnie's death," Mike said. "I didn't mention it because I found nothing, and I didn't want to alarm the rest of the party."

Pauline nodded and continued warming on the stove a pan of French Canadian – according to the can's label – split pea and ham soup. It looked remarkably like the same soup she'd loved growing up in England.

"You must suspect someone," Mike persisted.

"Oh, I'm sure we all suspect someone," Pauline replied coolly.

"The one that bothers me," Mike said, lowering his voice and carefully looking around to be sure no one was near, "is Jo. She and Arnie looked high on something that night."

"They were," Pauline replied. "Probably what people call

'uppers' but I'd say it was the more readily available ones, rather than hard drugs."

"The disco scene drugs," Mike said.

"Exactly. The ones that help you dance all night and still get up for work next morning."

"So you don't think it significant?" Mike asked.

"It concerns me, particularly as we now know she was questioned by the police about drug possession years ago," Pauline said. "Perhaps she never gave them up. Perhaps she just got cleverer at hiding them."

"I'd thought it was Arnie who brought them," Mike admitted.

"And he may have done," Pauline said. "We've no reason to think Jo did. In my time with Neufeldt, I've never seen any signs of drug-taking by her or any one of our partners."

"That's a relief," Mike said. "You probably have more experience of that kind of thing than I have."

"Not as much as you might imagine," Pauline said. "I don't get involved in sordid cases, if I can help it, and drugs are always sordid."

"What about Saul?"

"What about him?" Pauline asked. "There's no evidence he even knew Arnie before today, except by reputation perhaps."

"I can't see the two kids being involved, can you?"

"They can't have known Arnie and they barely knew Bryan," Pauline said, "and if Bryan was a mistake because they wanted to kill me, it's even less likely because I didn't know John until I arrived here, and Tom is as new here as I am. It seems highly unlikely is all I can say right now."

"That only leaves Gilles, me, and the Pomerleaus."

Pauline hoped he wasn't going to push the Pomerleau line of thought for she hadn't shared the conversation she'd overheard and didn't want to right now. Catrina or Laurent Pomerleau were both very much on her mind as possible murderers of Arnie. After all, Arnie was the one nearest in age to Catrina and likely to have been a young man in Toronto when Catrina was training there. But why would Catrina choose to kill Bryan, or was that a mistake and it was meant for Pauline? Was it because Pauline might stumble on the truth? Had they realized she must have overheard the conversation and decided to get rid of her before the police arrived?

"So, you do think it's one of us then?" Mike said, interpreting her long silence as confirmation.

"No more than I suspect Jo and Saul," Pauline replied. She smiled. "With the exception of you, of course."

"I'm glad to hear it," Mike said, grinning. "You knew Gilles before. Can you think of a reason why he might want to kill Arnie?"

"Not really, but he was as angry as I was at Arnie's behavior all those years ago. Maybe there was more to it than just disgust. And maybe he decided my investigation was too much of a risk for him to allow it to continue. Unfortunately for whoever it was, Bryan got the poison meant for me."

"It was certainly unfortunate for Bryan," Mike said wryly. "Are you sure about the poison and where it might have come from?"

"Not sure. As I said to Inspector Ormiston, I suspect it's curarine, or curare, and you can get it from hospitals where it's used in small doses for muscular problems and anesthesia purposes but I'm not an expert on poisons."

"You can't just walk into a hospital, take it from a cupboard, and walk out with it," Mike said. "I've never heard of Gilles or anyone volunteering in a hospital, have you?"

"No, but then there may be other ways to get it. Drug stores, perhaps. I don't really know. I'm hoping Inspector Ormiston will learn of any place that's short of some."

"Speaking of Ormiston," Mike said, "eat up quick. We should be calling him in ten minutes."

"No new murders, Miss Riddell?" Ormiston asked when they finally connected.

"Thankfully no, Inspector," Pauline replied. "Have you anything new?"

"I haven't found where the poison came from if that's what you're hoping for."

"That's disappointing, Inspector," Pauline said. "Is it because none has been reported missing or that you haven't been round to every drug store and hospital?"

Ormiston laughed. "The latter, Miss Riddell. We're buried in snow down here too, you know."

"I do understand, Inspector," Pauline said. "It's just frustrating when we can't get a grasp on who's done this. People are scared."

"I know. I do have some other information that is equally frustrating. John Beresford's mother died recently. She was American born, but beyond that they have little else to share."

"The radio news says the weather down in the northern states is awful too," Pauline said.

"Yes, we're all snowed under, if you'll pardon the pun."

Pauline laughed. "Not willingly, but I will if you keep researching for me. I wondered if she lived here in Canada when John was born."

"Canada is a big place," Ormiston said. "Asking for the birth records of a John Beresford around twenty-five years ago and expecting an answer by today, is a tall order."

"I know. Nothing new has come up on anyone else?"

"Nope. When will LaPlante get there?"

"He'd hoped today but we have had another ice storm so maybe tomorrow."

"Then we're luckier than you," Ormiston replied. "Here the sun is shining and we're getting back to normal. Take care, Miss Riddell."

Pauline assured him she would and ended the transmission. Turning to Mike she said, "When you were gathering information for recruiting John, didn't you learn anything that might help?"

Mike shook his head. "I told you. I was only concerned about his work and his reputation. Why?"

"He's the one we know so little about, that's all."

"We know as much about him as the others, at least with regard to his police record," Mike said. "He hasn't got one. Not here and not in the States."

Pauline nodded. "That's true but not knowing more is frustrating."

"Why? The police haven't found more about him because of the cross-border complication and the bad weather hampering their research, that's all."

"You're probably right," Pauline said, as they headed back into the house. "I'm a bit like a dog with a bone, gnawing at it even though all the meat is gone."

"You're worried about *not* knowing more about John," Mike said, quietly. "I'm worried about what I *learned* about Jo and how it jives with what I saw that night."

As they ascended the stairs, Pauline said, "And we're both probably way off the mark. That's my experience. It's always the one I didn't suspect – until I do."

"Then it's probably Tom," Mike said, grinning. "Though you'd have to provide some truly compelling evidence for me to believe that." He signaled Gilles to join them so he wouldn't be alone with Pauline nor her with him.

"Evidence, no," Pauline said, "but I have an idea."

"Tell me."

Seeing Gilles was still some way off on the stairs, Pauline shook her head and said quietly, "Look at how worried you've become about Jo. It wouldn't be fair to share my ideas with you about anyone else." She paused, as she opened her room door and stepped inside. Then she grinned, and added, "Except maybe about you." She closed the door behind her.

"What idea?" Mike called, trying to open the door, which she'd already barricaded with the furniture.

"It was a joke, Mike," she said, smiling. "Clearly, I'm not very good at jokes."

"What idea, Mike?" Gilles said as he joined Mike outside Pauline's room door.

"Nothing," Mike said shortly. Then, seeing the frown appearing on Gilles face, he said, "Sorry. Pauline just suggested she had some ideas about how I could be the murderer and it took me by surprise. I guess I'd assumed I was above suspicion and her joke bothered me."

"None of us are above suspicion," Gilles said, not turning to leave. He raised his voice, "I'm sure Pauline can prove exactly how I did it."

"Not prove," Pauline replied, laughing, "at least, not yet."

# 29

## COMMUNICATIONS CUT

When Gilles had followed Mike and Pauline upstairs, Tom took the opportunity to say to those remaining in the lounge, "John and I have been talking about what we've all said before. Mike and Pauline should not be getting information from the police about the rest of us when we don't know the same things about them. We should do something about it."

"There's nothing we can do to stop it, though, is there," Saul replied.

"We can snip wires to the radio," Tom said.

"That would be easy to fix, surely," Jo said.

"Not if we snapped them inside the radio," John said. "As a kid, I played with radios a lot."

"They would stop us," Jo replied, considering the possibilities.

"Not if you two kept Gilles and Mike talking upstairs while Tom and I sabotaged the radio," John said.

"It certainly bugs me the way they talk to the police and tell us nothing of what is being said," Jo said. "How long do you need?"

"Ten minutes max," John said, grinning. He was clearly relishing this piece of anti-authority mischief.

"Ten minutes!" Saul cried, looking slightly alarmed. "What could we say that would take that long?"

Jo jumped to her feet. "We march up there and demand she tells us what they have on us, and we refuse to leave until they do. Come on." She strode off to the stairs with Saul hurrying behind her.

Tom and John crept forward as unobtrusively as they could until they could see Jo and Saul arriving on the upper landing and marching down the corridor.

"We've had enough," they heard Jo say.

John swiftly and quietly crossed the hall with Tom in his wake. They stopped at the kitchen door to confirm the Pomerleaus weren't inside working and passed on to the door leading into the garage.

"It's freezing," Tom whispered as they made their way to the truck.

"It will only take a minute," John said. "You stand look-out." He opened the truck door, slid under the steering wheel and dashboard, and felt around with his outstretched hands behind the dash. "Got it," he said. There followed a snapping sound and then another.

John slid back out, straightened his clothes, saying, "They won't be using that again any time soon."

They strode quickly back inside, quietly returning to the lounge, hearing the loud altercation going on upstairs.

"How are we going to tell them we're done," Tom said, grinning. "Sounds like they're set in for the day."

"They're having fun," John said. "Or at least Jo is. It will fill in their afternoon harmlessly enough and we can play some pool without having them trying to take the table."

"Good plan," Tom said. "Let's go."

While John and Tom were sabotaging the radio, Pauline felt her head was ringing, with all the loud voices, even though the gang were on the other side of the door. She refused every demand from Jo and Saul to be told what the police had shared but it had no effect. Mike and Gilles, who seemed to be trying to calm the situation, were making it worse. To every argument they made, Jo or Saul countered with a renewed, and louder, demand for the information.

Pauline knew her fellow guests' nerves were approaching breaking point, but she hadn't understood how much. Her call today with Ormiston had clearly been the snapping point. She considered telling them she wouldn't contact the police again, but a breakthrough was needed. Ormiston was her best hope for that.

Eventually they left, and Pauline was able to return to her notes. She was badly shaken by the unpleasantness of the incident, and it took a moment before she could concentrate on her latest memories of what Ormiston had said on the call. Eventually, calm was restored to her mind and ideas flowed as she considered every possibility. One thing stood out; she needed to speak to Catrina Pomerleau alone. That overheard conversation was looking ever more important. But how could she make that happen? In their present mood, she was sure the others wouldn't accept it.

Had Catrina snapped and killed Arnie? Maybe Arnie had recognized her and been his usual insensitive self and that had driven her over the edge. Maybe it had driven Laurent, not Catrina, over the edge. Pauline read the notes she'd made during and after the interviews she'd had with them. She checked her watch. In an hour, she'd hammer on the door to ask for a mid-afternoon tea and have Mike escort her down to the kitchen to prepare it.

Downstairs, Mike, Gilles, Jo, and Saul joined John and Tom in the games room.

Tom straightened up from taking his shot and asked, "Did you get answers?"

"We didn't," Jo replied. "We're still treated as would-be murderers while the most likely murderer collects data to frame us with."

"That's not true," Mike said. "You must stop talking and thinking this way. Pauline is an experienced investigator and will get to the bottom of these terrible murders sooner than anyone else could."

"Mike," Saul said, "you can't expect us all to have the confidence in her you seem to have. We barely know her, and the evidence suggests she did these things."

"Guys," Gilles said, "we wouldn't accept any of this in our audit reports. There is *no* real evidence Pauline had a hand in either killing. In fact, she was most likely to be the intended victim in the second one."

"You both talk as if people can't go off the rails," John said. "There are plenty of examples of people who've led an exemplary life suddenly, and without warning, committing crimes. All it needs is a strong enough motive."

"And what motive could Pauline have?" Mike asked exasperatedly.

"We don't know," Jo said, "which is why we want a neutral researcher to sift for the evidence. Not the perpetrator guiding the investigation away from themselves."

"Pauline will continue to investigate until the police get here. That's final," Mike said. "Now, find something else to occupy your minds because this isn't helping."

There was a sullen silence at this, only Tom and John who were continuing their game seemed willing to let it drop.

"Gilles, can we talk?" Mike said, gesturing toward his office.

When they left, the games room remained silent for a few minutes. Then Jo said, "I suggest we take shifts watching her door tonight. Whatever it is she's doing may not be over and I don't like the idea that Mike has the only key to her room. What if he hasn't?"

"You know," John said. "I wondered about that. What if there was a fire or some other emergency? I don't believe Mike would have left it that she couldn't escape from her room."

"Exactly," Jo cried, triumphantly. "So who agrees with me about watching tonight?"

The others looked at each other. "Do you mean alone?" Saul asked.

"Why not?" Jo said. "I know I didn't kill anyone so having a partner with me makes me *more* nervous, not less."

Tom laughed. "I didn't like to say anything, being the new kid on the block and all, but that's exactly how I've felt the whole time."

John grinned. "Hear, hear. I thought no one would ever say it."

"I'll take the second shift," Saul said. "I've not been sleeping so well since Arnie was murdered. I may as well do something useful with my insomnia."

"I'll go first," Jo said. "There are four of us and we're looking at around eight hours. Two hours each isn't too hard."

"Okay," Tom said, "but I want the last shift because if people get up early, it will be a short one." He grinned, pleased at his cleverness.

"I guess that leaves the graveyard shift for me," John said. "What times are we looking at?"

They quickly set out a roster for the night and were back to playing pool and darts by the time Mike and Gilles returned.

# 30

# AT LAST, REAL SUSPECTS

By mid-afternoon, when she felt sufficient time had passed for tempers to cool, Pauline called for attention and, when Mike and Gilles arrived, she explained she had to talk to Catrina and Laurent again.

"You suspect them?" Gilles asked.

Pauline hesitated. Could she share with these two what she'd overheard? She'd ruled them out as likely objects of Catrina's dislike but only because of the difference in ages between them and Catrina. She now decided that wasn't reason enough. After all, older men were often found in the company of younger women.

"I just want to talk with them some more about Arnie and particularly with Catrina about the teapot."

"They won't like it," Mike said.

"I know but I must try. Can you fix it with them?"

"I want to be there with you," Mike said. "They're neighbors and friends. We've known each other for decades."

"Very well," Pauline said, hoping this would be the least of their demands. "Arrange it."

Twenty minutes later, Mike and Gilles escorted Pauline

into the kitchen where the Pomerleaus were waiting. Their postures said more clearly than words how much they resented this.

"I'll leave you guys to it," Gilles said to Mike and Pauline. He walked away to join the others in the games room, which had become the group's permanent daytime retreat.

"Catrina," Pauline said. "I must ask you something very personal. Please believe I wouldn't do this if I didn't have to."

"You can ask," Catrina said. "I can't promise to answer."

"Before all this began, I overheard you and Laurent talking. You said 'I can't keep out of his way forever' or something very like that. Who did you mean?"

Catrina and Laurent exchanged glances. Laurent shrugged. Taking this as a sign he was okay with her elaborating, Catrina said, "Arnie Hamilton. He was a sharp talker, even as a young man."

"You met him when you were a student in Toronto?"

She nodded. "The teacher's training college I attended was right next to the university he was at. We met at a party, and we went out together for some weeks."

"You fell out?"

"He was a bully," Catrina said. "We didn't so much fall out, as I stopped seeing him. He took it badly and stalked and harassed me for weeks after that. In the end, I got the college authorities involved and they spoke to the university management."

"That was the end of it?"

"Not entirely," Catrina said. "He didn't approach or speak to me again, which is what he'd agreed, but unpleasant things happened for the rest of that college year. I knew it was him, but I couldn't prove anything. Then I heard he got a new girlfriend over the summer break, and the harassment didn't continue the next semester. I was a lot more careful about parties after that, as you might imagine."

"I can imagine," Pauline said sympathetically. "You didn't consider leaving the college, transferring to another one away from him?"

"Why should I?" Catrina said. "I thought that, like all bullies, he was a coward at heart. I didn't fear for my life or anything."

"You have more courage than me," Pauline said, smiling. "I would certainly have requested a move."

"I hear you investigate murders, so I suspect that isn't entirely true, Miss Riddell," Catrina said.

There was a steely quality to her voice Pauline found both disconcerting and re-assuring. Like many – perhaps most – everyday folks, she had reserves of courage that only showed when danger threatened. Her explanation appeared honest and forthright, without a suggestion of wanting revenge. Still, Pauline mused, if Arnie had been his usual self on recognizing her and she'd thought such an opportunity could not be missed, she might well have the nerve to take it. And if she didn't, was Laurent so lacking in passion he wouldn't take the chance to punish someone who'd wronged his wife?

"Did you know Catrina when this happened, Laurent?"

Laurent's angry expression turned almost at once to near fury. "So, you can't get Catrina to confess to killing him and you decide to finger me?"

"I'm only trying to eliminate possibilities," Pauline said. "And if you're upset at my questioning, how will you manage when the police ask?"

"They have the right to ask," Laurent said. "You don't."

"We all have the right to ask questions," Pauline said, "and I do understand your anger. After all, every one of my fellow guests is accusing me of murder and it upsets me too."

"Then why aren't you questioning them?" Laurent said. "Or are they too clever and professional for murder. It must be working people who did it."

"That's nonsense and you know it is. Neither you nor Catrina are abused workers and my fellow guests are hardly royalty. I've interviewed them and followed up with them more than once."

Laurent seemed to pull himself together and reply more calmly, "Yeah, sorry. That came out all wrong."

"Well, did you have any dealings with Arnie Hamilton before he turned up here on Friday?"

Laurent shook his head, but it was Catrina who answered. "I told Laurent who Arnie was, the moment I saw him," she said. "I saw him through the kitchen window when he was getting out of his car. I recognized him at once, you see, and Laurent saw me react. He asked me what was the matter. I thought it better to tell him the truth rather than a lie that he wouldn't have fallen for."

"When you learned about Arnie, Laurent, were you angry enough to intend him harm?"

"I was disgusted, not angry," Laurent said. "We were all young and stupid once. He didn't harm Catrina, or it might have been different. I can understand being young and in love. We've all felt angry at a breakup, and I thought that's all that happened."

"Did either of you confront him?" Pauline asked, glancing from Catrina to Laurent.

They shook their heads.

"Catrina?" Pauline pressed.

"No, I kept in the background and then he was dead. There was no chance to meet."

In response to Pauline turning to him, Laurent said. "After Catrina told me who he was, I met him when I was carrying in his baggage and that was in the company of Mike and Gilles who'd come out to greet him. There, you have it. We both have a thin motive and, as we can wander the house at will, we had the opportunity. As well, like they say on TV detective shows, I had the means to do it too because I put away everyone's ski baggage in the mud room."

"I see you've thought about this," Pauline said, smiling.

"Of course, we have," Catrina said. "There was always a good chance the police would learn about my history with Hamilton, even though it never came to their attention all those years ago. We needed to get our stories straight."

"Then I'm pleased I could help you deliver them," Pauline said wryly. "Did your stories go as you meant them too?"

They clearly weren't pleased at her gentle, mocking tone for they both flushed pink.

"We've told you the truth and it's what we'll tell the police when they ask," Catrina said, flatly. "Now, unless you have any more questions, we'll get back to our room."

"Just one more question," Pauline said. "Do either of you volunteer at the local hospital?"

They shook their heads.

"Laurent, you're the local handyman, do you do work there?" Pauline asked.

"I have done," Laurent said, "but not recently. Why?"

"I'm wondering about the tea that killed Bryan," Pauline said. "Perhaps it was a poison from a drug store or hospital."

"I work in the local drug store when they're shorthanded," Catrina said, "but I don't dispense drugs and I've no idea what any of them do, except for the common ones."

“How do you think something could have gotten into the tea?”

“Search me,” Catrina said. “I put the teabags in the pot, poured boiling water on them and took the pot out to the breakfast room when I heard you were coming down. A more puzzling question is why didn’t you drink it after all the fuss you made over only drinking tea?”

“Honestly, I don’t know,” Pauline said. “I was reaching for the pot and then thought, ‘I’ll need a whole lot more caffeine to sort through this puzzle’ and I took coffee instead.”

“Sound unlikely to me,” Laurent said. “Will the police buy it, do you think?”

“It even sounds unlikely to me,” Pauline said, ruefully, “and I suspect they *won’t* buy it. But it’s what happened.”

“Anything else?” Catrina asked.

“Not right now,” Pauline said. “Thanks for your help.”

The Pomerleaus moved as one toward the outside door and Pauline and Mike were left alone.

When they’d closed the door behind them, Mike said, “Did you believe them?”

Pauline nodded. “I believe what they told us, but did they tell us everything that happened? That’s the bit I can’t pin down.”

“Laurent’s point about the tea is a good one,” Mike said. “You may want to find a better explanation.”

“It’s what happened,” Pauline said. “In the end, I believe we should stick to that and let the process take its course.”

“I like your confidence in natural justice,” Mike said, as they left the kitchen, “but I fear legal justice is often tripped up by oddities such as your sudden coffee whim.”

“Then I must trust my good character references,” Pauline said, smiling.

"Seriously, though, Pauline, are you really no nearer solving this?"

"Solving it, yes," Pauline said. "Proving it, not so much."

"You think it was the Pomerleaus? A spur of the moment murder and then an attempt to silence you when they realized you were a successful investigator?"

"I didn't say who I believe is the culprit," Pauline replied calmly. "Only I'm almost sure I know who is. I'm also sure tonight will be the perpetrator's last chance to silence me. You'd better be ready for trouble."

Mike nodded. "They can't think silencing you will prevent the police discovering the truth, can they?"

"I think the motive is more than just silence," Pauline said. "Now, I should return to my room and you to your guests. We will talk again at supper time."

As they walked across the hall to the broad staircase leading up to the bedrooms, Pauline grinned at the anxious faces watching them. No one spoke. Gilles, however, left the group and joined Pauline and Mike on the stairs.

"Can't have you running around unchaperoned, Mike," he said, grinning.

"True," Mike said. "Pauline might murder me at any moment, or I might murder her. You never can tell in these matters."

"Have you considered that, using my judo and karate training, I might kill both of you?" Pauline said.

"You watch too many movies," Gilles said.

"If it makes you feel safer," Pauline replied, smiling, "it's been a long time since I did any of that stuff." She paused, as they arrived at her bedroom door and Mike unlocked it. "Gentlemen, thank you for walking me home. Your concern does you great credit."

She entered her bedroom, closing the door behind her.

When she heard the key turn in the lock, and the men walking away, she pushed the dresser back across the door.

When Mike and Gilles arrived back downstairs, they were immediately accosted by the others demanding to know what the Pomerleaus had said and why Pauline thought they did it.

"Pauline doesn't think they did anything," Mike replied, "or not that I know of. She hasn't taken me into her confidence."

"Then why question them again?" Jo asked.

"Pauline just wanted clarification about something that had been said earlier," Mike explained.

"They did it though, didn't they?" Saul said.

"Why would you think that?"

"She wouldn't have made all that fuss unless there was something big behind it. She spotted something in their statement and now she's sure, right?" Saul asked.

"It was nothing like that," Mike said, with a sigh that said he wished this was all over.

"Then what was it like?" Tom asked. "Not being told anything, when we're as much involved as anyone in all this, is driving me nuts."

"The police will be here tomorrow and then everything will be in their hands," Mike said. "They will make any arrests and then you'll know."

"We could all be dead by then," Jo cried.

"How?" Gilles asked, exasperated. "Unless you're saying the murderer is one of us. Pauline is locked in."

"She can get to the kitchen for meals and out to the garage to the radio," Saul pointed out. "She'll find a way if she wants to."

"And why should she want to?" Mike asked. "Pauline has no reason to kill anyone here. She didn't have a reason to kill Arnie or Bryan, either. This is madness. You're letting your brains run wild down some strange rabbit holes."

"Madness! Two people are dead," Saul cried. "She is implicated in both. We may not know her reasons but that means we don't know if any of us are next on her list."

Mike shook his head. "Enough," he said. "Enough. Pauline is locked in her room. We keep together until morning when the police arrive. That way we're all safe, no matter who is the murderer."

"Or murderers," Tom said. "You're forgetting the Pomerleaus. And they control the kitchen and the house heating. They have the run of the place."

"We're safe if we stick together," Gilles said. "And we only eat out of cans and drink bottled water. By this time tomorrow, it'll all be over."

The group lapsed once again into sullen silence, which alarmed Gilles more than their anger did.

"Let's vote for a video to watch," he suggested, getting a chorus of groans in reply.

"We've watched the ones we can all agree on," John said.

"Then we watch the one with the most votes," Gilles replied. "I'll read the titles. Jo, you count the votes."

"Mike has terrible taste in movies," Saul grumbled as the voting began.

"A lot are for my nephews and nieces," Mike admitted. "I don't watch movies much."

"I should hope not," Gilles said, grinning, "at least not these ones."

"And how come you're still on the old Betamax system," Tom teased. "I thought even old people had graduated to VHS by now."

"Less of the old people, kid," Mike said. "I bought that

machine when they first came out and it still runs as good as new."

"Betamax don't get the new movies anymore," John said. "We could have watched *Witness*; it might have helped us solve the murder."

Gilles shook his head. "*Clue* is what we need. Why don't you have that one, Mike?"

"I'm too busy to watch movies, new or old," Mike retorted, "and my nephews and nieces like the old stuff I have anyhow."

As Gilles read the titles of each children's movie, the comments grew more jocular, and the tension that had gripped them slipped away. By the time they'd settled on an old Western, *The Sons of Katie Elder*, it felt something like normality had returned.

## 31

# INCOMMUNICADO

UPSTAIRS, Pauline walked to the window and looked out. The storm was easing off. Perhaps the police would be able to arrive in the morning, as she so dearly wished. It was a source of pride for her that she'd often unmasked a murderer before the police did, and she'd more than once acted as the tethered goat to bring the tiger out of its lair, only this time it was too near to home. The killer had meant for her to die almost from the start and had killed the unfortunate Bryan instead.

She walked to the bedside table where a clock-radio-alarm took up much of the space. It was curious, she thought, that whoever put in the generator had hooked it to the bedside lamps and clocks; obviously, they thought them essential. Switching it on, she flicked through the stations hoping to catch a weather report. As always, all she got were advertisements, which she hated. She switched back to the local Canadian Broadcasting Corporation station and left it there. It would take time but eventually there would be a weather forecast and at least there'd be fewer advertisements.

By the time Mike and Gilles came to collect her for her evening meal, she'd heard what she wanted to hear. The weather was set fair for overnight and the following day, which meant the police should arrive.

As the three walked down the stairs, Pauline was conscious something was different this time. She looked about but she saw nothing to make her uneasy as they crossed the hall to the kitchen where it was clear she was the only one who liked French Canadian Pea and Ham soup for there were always cans of that available. She would have liked some French Canadian tourtiere as well. She'd seen a frozen tourtiere pie in the freezer earlier in the weekend, but at this stage she felt safer just opening solid cans.

When she'd finished eating, they left the kitchen and headed out to the truck. It took some time to realize the radio wasn't just acting up, it was dead.

"The only ones who could have wrecked it are Laurent and Catrina," Mike said. "The rest of us have been together all afternoon."

As Mike was speaking, Pauline realized what had been wrong when she'd come down the stairs. Every other time, the angry, vengeful eyes of her fellow guests had watched her. This time, they'd all been absent.

"You weren't together all afternoon," she said. "When you, Gilles, Jo, and Saul were ranting outside my door, Tom and John weren't there."

Mike swore softly. "You're right," he said. "One of them did it. Does that mean they did the murders too?"

"Not necessarily," Pauline said. "They're all incensed at us talking to the police without them. They could all be behind it. Jo and Saul provided cover while Tom and John slipped outside and wrecked the radio. It may not even have been Tom and John's idea."

"I hope the police do get here tomorrow; things are getting out of hand."

"The weather's improving," Pauline said. "They should be here in the morning. I'll also be very glad of it."

"You still think the murderer will try to kill you?"

Pauline smiled. "I'm sure they'll try," she said. "What frightens me is I may have to kill them and that would put me in very badly with the law."

"Self-defense, surely," Mike said.

"Our laws are so backward now, no one is safe. Now we must return to what I'm sure will be an amused audience."

They left the garage, hung up their coats and re-entered the house. Pauline was right. There'd been no one to witness their descent of the stairs but everyone was there to watch them go back up.

"Any good news on the CB?" Jo said, hardly hiding her amusement.

"None, as I'm sure you all know," Pauline said.

"If we can't know about you," John said, "it's only fair you shouldn't know about us."

Pauline paused, looked at him and said, "You're all too late for that. I know all your secrets and the local police will know them too when they arrive tomorrow. Even the schoolboy stuff of you and Tom."

Tom flushed red, making Pauline wonder what it was she and the police *didn't* know about him.

"You're not worried telling us this will lead someone to attack you tonight?" Gilles asked, concerned, as they continued up the stairs.

"I have a small automatic pistol. I'm a very good shot," Pauline said. "And I don't plan to sleep tonight."

As Pauline entered her room and heard the door close behind her, she wondered if she'd made the bait too obvious. It was one thing to tell the perpetrator you know what they did and you're going to tell the police at the first opportunity. It was quite another to make it sound believable.

# 32

## COMMUNICATION RESTORED

On the following morning, Wednesday, after escorting Pauline back to her room from breakfast, Mike and Gilles joined the others in the kitchen where they were moodily drinking and holding a desultory conversation about movies, sport, and politics. There was no passion in their voices; it was as if each realized the conversation could become an argument if the wrong word was spoken; the tension was that thick.

The phone rang and everyone jumped. The sound was startling in the quiet. Mike strode quickly to the phone and picked it up.

"Hello?" he said. Then listened, before saying, "Thanks for letting me know." He replaced the handset.

"They've repaired the lines," he said. "We can talk to the outside world again."

There was an instant clamor of voices demanding to be first, which he quelled with a raised hand.

"Ladies first," he said. "Jo, the phone in my office is private. Maybe someone can go with you to keep you safe."

"I'll do that," Saul said, jumping to his feet.

"Good. Thanks, Saul," Mike replied. "Gilles, you and I can get Pauline. I'm sure she has plenty of people she needs to call." He'd expected some resistance to this from Tom and John but there wasn't any. Maybe the knowledge they could all call out had lowered their resentment.

Jo and Saul headed for the office, while Mike and Gilles returned upstairs. Mike knocked on the door.

"Who is it?" Pauline asked.

"Me, Mike. Did you hear? We have a phone line again."

"I didn't," Pauline said. "I need to call Ormiston and LaPlante, and as it's a workday, Jerry Seaforth will be in the office at Seaforth."

"I felt sure you'd have a list," Mike said, grinning. He unlocked the door.

"Jo's using the phone right now," Mike said as Pauline joined him in the corridor. "You can call after she's done."

"As long as she isn't on there all day," Pauline said sharply.

"I thought it was only men who said things like that," Gilles said, with an innocent expression.

"Your office isn't next to hers," Pauline replied. "Believe me, she *can* talk all day."

"We'll call time on it if it goes too long," Mike said. "Right now, we need to get everyone who wants to make a call the chance to do so."

Pauline's sharp comment was proved to be incorrect for by the time they'd arrived at Mike's office door, they found Jo had handed the line over to Saul. Mike frowned at this rule breaking, and his dark expression had Saul quickly wrapping up his call.

Pauline closed the door behind her when Saul left the office. Her first call was to Seaforth and Partners, her previous employer. When the phone was answered, she asked to be put through to Jerry Seaforth and was told by Jerry's secretary, Renata, Jerry was out.

"Renata, it's me, Pauline Riddell. Would you do me a favor?"

"What sort of favor?" Renata asked suspiciously.

"I need information about an audit I took part in with Arnie Hamilton way back in 1980. The first I did for Seaforth."

"You don't work here anymore, Pauline," Renata said. "I don't think Jerry will like me doing this without her say-so. I must check this with her."

"Okay, do that," Pauline said. "I'm not asking for any secrets, just the names of the guys the report named as being involved in criminal activity. There were three of them and I want to know their names. Please, it's important. Find the names and clear it with Jerry the moment she gets back. Call me as soon as you can." After giving Renata the number, and asking briefly about Renata's family and the people in the office, Pauline hung up.

Her next call was to Ormiston, leaving a message letting him know they could now talk by phone. Finally, she called LaPlante and found he too wasn't immediately available, and she had to leave a message there as well.

Dissatisfied, Pauline left the office and re-joined Gilles and Mike in the hall.

"Okay?" Mike asked.

Pauline grimaced. "The two inspectors are out of the office. I had to leave messages. I couldn't get Jerry at Seaforth and her secretary wants to check with the boss before releasing me any information. Not exactly what I was hoping for."

"You can't blame the secretary," Mike said. "I wouldn't

like information being handed out to non-employees either."

"It isn't Renata I'm unhappy with," Pauline said. "It's life. We finally have the means to communicate quickly and there's no one there to communicate with. It's a metaphor for the modern world, only I don't quite know what it's telling me."

"That you're not the center of the universe?" Gilles said with a laugh.

Pauline smiled. "I'm the center of my universe and that universe is looking shaky right now," she replied tartly.

"You don't really think the police will believe it was you, do you?" Mike asked.

"I don't, but it is preying on my mind," Pauline said. "They have to follow the evidence and I haven't found any new evidence to contradict what's up there in the bedrooms, have I?"

"The forensic folks will find plenty, I'm sure," Gilles said.

Pauline nodded. "I certainly hope so or I'm in for a difficult time for the next days, maybe even weeks."

"You've really no idea?"

"I think I do, and if Renata supplies me some names, I think that will solve it," Pauline said. "If not, I'll have to have Ormiston or LaPlante get the names."

"Can I help?" Gilles asked. "I worked there too."

Pauline hesitated. "It was the audit I did with Arnie, Gilles. Do you remember the names of the men we identified as being involved in criminal activity?"

Gilles took a moment to think before saying, "No, sorry, I can't say I do. It was too long ago. We've done lots of similar audits since then."

Further discussion was ended when Tom and John

approached them. Tom asked, "If you're finished with the phone, can the rest of us call out now?"

Mike nodded. "I forgot. Sorry guys. Yes, go ahead." He turned to Pauline. "I guess we should get you back to your room," he said.

Pauline nodded. "If any of my three contacts call back, you'll get me at once, won't you?"

"Of course," Mike said, leading the way toward the stairs. "How are we going to stop others listening in on the phones in the lounge and games room though? That's the problem."

"You guard one, I'll guard the other," Gilles said. "You can lock Pauline in your office while we do that."

"The others won't like it," Mike said.

"It can't be helped," Gilles replied. "One of them is the murderer and we can't have them listening in and learning we know who it is."

"I'll collect you around twelve-thirty, Pauline," Mike said, as he was unlocking her bedroom door, "unless you get an earlier call back."

# 33

# PREVENTING ESCAPE

THE CALL CAME LATE MORNING. Mike knocked on Pauline's door and told her to come quickly. Jerry Seaforth was on the phone.

Pauline had been waiting and was ready to go. She, Mike, and Gilles made their way quickly down the stairs in what Pauline hoped would be the last of these chaperoned events.

She closed the office door firmly behind her, leaving Mike and Gilles to guard the phones in the other rooms.

"Hello, Jerry," Pauline said, seating herself in Mike's office chair.

"Pauline," Jerry replied neutrally. Their relationship had never been cordial, and Pauline's leaving the firm had reduced it further.

"Do you have the names?" Pauline asked.

"Why do you want them?"

Pauline explained, omitting that she was suspected of both killings. She didn't feel that would be helpful at this stage.

"How do you get yourself into these situations?" Jerry

asked. "Most people never figure in any murder investigation."

"Most people aren't asked to become part of one," Pauline said. "Still, I take your point."

"I imagine the police are involved with these murders, so why aren't they asking?"

"They are involved," Pauline said, frustrated at Jerry's delaying tactics. "It's just we've been cut-off by the storms. We had no phones until this morning. We expect them here tomorrow morning. I'll give them the names right now, and why I think they're important. That way they can do some background before they get here."

"Maybe I should wait for you to call them and them to call me," Jerry said.

"Jerry, I'm not asking for anything secret. I have a copy of the audit back at my apartment. If I could have gotten the police to find these names, I would have done, but we haven't been able to talk to anyone for days."

There was a long pause and then Jerry said, "Very well. Here they are."

To Pauline's dismay, the names, at first glance, didn't help. None of the three family names lined up with people in the lodge. Pauline frowned. She'd been sure she had the answer at last and it seemed she didn't.

"It's always darkest before dawn," she said softly.

"What does that mean?" Jerry asked.

"I was talking to myself, sorry," Pauline replied. "Thanks, Jerry. I owe you."

"You don't," Jerry said. "You solved Lynnette's murder and eased Dad's last days. That counts for a lot with me."

*Strange you never showed it then*, Pauline thought but said, "I was happy to help. I really liked your father. He was a good man."

"A good man whose life was marred by terrible personal tragedies," Jerry said. "How can that be fair. Your God seems to go missing sometimes, I think."

"It's a problem that thinkers have grappled with since time began," Pauline said. "And it always comes back to *life isn't fair*. And it can't be made so, no matter how much we try."

"I think about Dad a lot now," Jerry said.

Pauline didn't know what to say. Whenever she thought about Ed it was how happy she'd been when he'd relented and let Jerry run Seaforth. She'd thought Ed unkind for robbing Jerry of her chance. When he reversed his decision, she'd hoped it would turn out well. It hadn't. In the end, Pauline had left Seaforth to join Neufeldt, the company which had allowed itself to be taken over. Ed had been hoping to save Seaforth by joining the global world and Jerry, and Pauline, had prevented that. But Ed had been right, and Pauline hadn't. Her own conscience in this unhappy sequence of events gave her many uncomfortable moments of contemplation.

"You do too, I think," Jerry said, when the silence had gone on too long.

"I do," Pauline said. "Your father had a talent for business as I have a talent for investigating. I set aside his expertise, as so many do mine. I regret that now. I should have had more faith."

Jerry laughed. "Churchgoers always think they should have more faith," she said.

"In this case, I meant faith in him and his talent, not in the eternal struggle for human destiny," Pauline said.

Jerry gave a short, harsh laugh. "I know what you meant. I hope your investigation goes well and," she paused, "I hope we meet again soon."

Pauline said what was needed and hung up the phone with very mixed feelings. Like she and Jo, she and Jerry had never gotten along. Perhaps it isn't possible for rivals in life to be friends; with that thought, she rose from the chair and headed toward the door.

She stopped, returned to the seat, and called Ormiston.

"Miss Riddell, how nice of you to call," he said sarcastically.

Pauline, who was used to his ways, said, "I have some names for you to run background checks on."

"Does it ever occur to you I may have a life that doesn't involve doing your legwork?"

"Inspector, this is serious," Pauline said. "Have you a pen and paper?"

"I have. Go ahead."

Pauline read the names she'd been given and asked, "When might you know?"

"I'll have someone look into these now," Ormiston said. "The afternoon and night shifts will love having something to do instead of just patrolling the streets. I may have something by later today. Who are these people anyhow?"

Pauline explained.

"It should be easy to learn about them then," Ormiston said. "After all, they will be in our system and the prison service's system. With luck, we might have something today. You think one of their family is in the lodge?"

"I do," Pauline said.

"But normal people's family members don't carry out vendettas against those who put their relations in prison. It's not like that. Not here anyhow."

"It's just one lead I'm working on," Pauline said. "It's new and I need to know more, and quickly. Every moment here my life is at risk."

"I remember you telling me you were used to that," Ormiston said.

"I am and I'm taking precautions. Still, it isn't the sort of thing I want to go on forever. I find I'm not so casual with my life these days."

"It's called maturity, Pauline," Ormiston said. "It's hit you later than most, that's all."

"Very amusing," Pauline said sharply. "And if I end up shooting someone in self-defense, you'll be a character witness, I hope?"

Ormiston laughed. "Let me get the records office started. We'll talk again at the usual time, unless I get something relevant more quickly."

Not entirely pleased that he hadn't given an assurance he would speak in her favor, Pauline rejoined Mike in the corridor.

"Well?" Mike asked, impatiently. "Have you the answer?"

Pauline shook her head.

"No!"

"Not yet," Pauline said. "It needs more work."

"Or it's another dead end," Mike said harshly. The disappointment at this failure of another theory seemed to crush him.

"Possibly," Pauline said, walking thoughtfully back to her room.

"Pauline," Mike said, "the police will be here soon, and you'll be their number one suspect. Your colleagues – our partners – will see to that."

"The police aren't so easily swayed," Pauline said, "though I agree it will be uncomfortable for a while."

"Uncomfortable?" Mike said.

"I'm very close now."

"Which only puts your life in further danger," Mike replied.

"The culprit knows their hope of having me locked away for life is almost gone at this point," Pauline said. "There'll either be one last attempt at killing me or they'll try to escape." She paused and continued, "Mike, do your snowmobiles have gas in them?"

"Sure. I was hoping we'd get some use out of them this weekend. Why?"

"I just wondered," Pauline said. "The murderer may want an escape route before, after or instead of killing me."

"I'll take Gilles and we'll empty them."

"Can you do it without being obvious?" Pauline asked. "I'd like the culprit to get far enough away to be unable to walk back before the police arrive, but not too far so the police can't find them."

"It might be tricky to guess that exactly," Mike said. "And also, tricky to do it secretly. I'll play it by ear."

"Maybe a work meeting with Gilles in your office last thing tonight," Pauline suggested, as she shut the door.

"The perpetrator could still stumble upon us going to or coming from the garage," Mike said. He turned to see Gilles at the top of the stairs. He signaled Gilles to come closer and, when he did, explained the plan.

As Pauline was finishing her evening meal, thinking how pleased she would be if she never ate pea soup again, the phone rang.

"It's for Miss Riddell," she heard Laurent Pomerleau call from the kitchen.

Hurrying into the kitchen with Mike, Pauline took the handset from Laurent and said, "Inspector Ormiston?" She found it hard to keep the excitement out of her voice.

"Good guess," Ormiston replied. "As I promised, it's easy

when someone is in the system." He quickly relayed the information.

Pauline listened carefully, while watching her two companions, Laurent and Mike, who were hoping to hear what was being said.

"Thank you, Inspector," Pauline said, at last. "You may take the rest of the day off." She laughed at his tart response and hung up the phone.

"Well?" Mike demanded.

"We stick to our plan, Mike," Pauline said, and returned to her now cold soup.

## 34

# ON THE RUN

By midnight, the house was quiet, even Gilles and Mike had gone to bed. In her room, Jo was dressed and waiting, ready to start her period of guard duty. She'd heard Mike and Gilles come upstairs. Their constant meetings, without her or Saul, bothered Jo a lot. She was certain they were talking about her and Saul in those meetings, and not to their advantage. Still, what was done was done, and she wasn't a person who looked often in the rear-view mirror. She cracked open her bedroom door, looked out both ways along the corridor and slipped quietly through the door.

She was wearing her thickest pants and sweater and held a lethal looking metal comb with a sharp pointed handle. Not the best weapon but the only one she could find without rousing suspicion. She pulled the door almost closed behind her and leaned against the jamb. Saul would relieve her in less than two hours, but it would seem much longer she knew.

Pauline rose from her bed and tiptoed to the door. She was sure she'd heard someone moving. She listened carefully but the sound wasn't repeated. Returning to her bed, she propped herself up on pillows against the headboard, placed the Beretta on her lap, and continued reading her new book, *The Handmaid's Tale*. It had been highly recommended to her, but it struck her as just more of the usual anti-religious posturing that was so fashionable now. She blamed the tele-evangelists for this sad situation. Still, she was persevering with it for she liked to believe she listened to both sides of any argument.

Nothing disturbed Pauline from inside the house. Outside, however, she heard snuffling and scratching and looked out to see deer milling around in the open space between the house and the trees. She loved deer, so elegant and gentle, watching them until they disappeared back into the bushes.

An hour later, she heard soft sounds in the corridor and again crept to the door to listen. A door closed, and the house was silent again. Pauline returned to her bed and waited. Was this the moment when the murderer tries to clean up the remaining loose end? Minutes turned to an hour and nothing new disturbed the house except some snoring farther along the corridor.

Sometime later, Pauline was jolted from her light nap by stealthy sounds of a door opening, soft footsteps, and a door closing. Was this the moment? She rose from the bed and stretched herself, shaking out the stiffness from her joints, before making her way quietly to the door. She pressed her ear to the door and heard the footsteps creep closer. The person outside was so close she could hear them breathing. She held her own breath, hoping not to be heard.

The footsteps moved on toward the stairs and she breathed easily again. She listened until she could no longer hear them. The murderer was now downstairs and doing what? They couldn't get into her room and couldn't get anything *into* the room either. She'd put a wet towel across the bottom of the door; no gas or other airborne poison could enter that way. Even if they had a key, the door was effectively blocked by the dresser. The window was too high for a casual intruder and the ice over everything outdoors would dissuade even the most accomplished cat burglar.

Noises outside took Pauline back to the window. Her view was restricted to the trees and lake. What she needed to see was the garage. She unlocked the window and pushed it open as far as she could. As she'd suspected, what she heard was the sound of garage doors opening. A moment later, an engine started. Then she heard the sound of a snowmobile moving out onto the snow. The roar of its motor rose, its headlight swept the trees to her right before disappearing, and then slowly the noise died away into the distance.

There was a knock on her bedroom door. "Pauline," she heard Mike call.

Pauline crossed to the door and said, "He took a snowmobile, as I thought he might."

"Gilles and I want to follow."

"Unlike the movie you all watched, this isn't the Wild West," Pauline said. "Here, if the posse shoots the bad guy, it's the posse who go to prison."

Mike growled his disapproval. "We know, which is why we didn't follow him."

"What we need to do," Pauline said, "is stop anyone eating anything this morning. We don't know if he had any curarine left and how or where he might have distributed it."

"Never thought of that. You're right," Mike said.

"Another thing we need to do is call through to LaPlante.

He could head the murderer off at the junction with the main road."

"Let me get you out first," Mike said.

Pauline heard the key turning in the lock as she removed the towel from the bottom of the door. The door tried to open before she said, "Wait."

She stood and slowly dragged the dresser away from the door.

"Okay, you can open it now."

Mike pushed the door open and stepped inside, stopping with a jolt. Pauline's automatic was pointed straight at his stomach.

"Hey," Mike said, "point that somewhere else."

"The safety catch is on," Pauline said, lowering the pistol now she could see he had nothing in his hands. She'd hardly noticed herself doing that, but it seemed her nerves were as strained as everyone else's. "Phone first," she said, slipping past them and racing along the corridor.

The phone, however, was dead.

"What is it?" Gilles asked, seeing her dismay.

"He cut the phone line before he left," Pauline said. "We need Laurent to fix his radio." She replaced the handset and set off toward the outer door.

"We should both go," Mike said, following her. "That way, the Pomerleaus will believe us better."

"I hope so. We need that radio working as soon as we can, and Laurent is our best hope for that."

Downstairs, Pauline and Gilles quickly closed the entrances to the kitchen, preventing any half-asleep guest entering, while Mike rushed off to rouse Laurent. Ten minutes later, a well-wrapped Laurent began working to repair the radio.

"Can it be fixed?" Mike asked, when Laurent had been unscrewing bolts under the dashboard for a few minutes.

"It's just snapped wiring," Laurent said, looking up to Mike from the truck floor. "I think it's fixable."

"How long?"

"It'll be quicker if you let me get on," Laurent said, grinning. He removed the radio from its bracket before sliding out from under the dash, sat on the driver's seat and unscrewed the cover, exposing the radio's innards.

"Yeah, sorry," Mike said, sheepishly. "I'll shut up." He turned away and began pacing the floor. He'd only done two turns the length of the garage when he saw Laurent replacing the radio's cover.

Turning the truck's ignition key brought on the radio's indicator lights. Laurent switched it on, and it crackled into life. He carefully placed the radio back in its holder, stepped away and said, "Get Miss Riddell here to talk to LaPlante."

Mike practically ran back into the house, calling for Pauline to come to the radio.

The police radio operator wasn't entirely convinced by her insistence he needed to bring LaPlante to the radio at four-thirty in the morning.

"We have a murderer escaping from the scene of the crime," Pauline said forcefully. "If you won't call LaPlante, at least get officers to the junction of highway eleven and sideroad twenty-five."

"Who is this calling?" the man asked.

"Pauline Riddell," Pauline replied. "LaPlante knows who I am."

The man laughed. "And I do too, Miss Riddell. I've been the one receiving and collating the background information from Inspector Ormiston. I'll get officers out there and get LaPlante as soon as I can."

Pauline sighed with relief. “Thank you,” she said. “I’ll leave this open so LaPlante can reach us the moment he’s available.”

She stepped out of the truck and, turning to Laurent, said, “Thanks for this, Laurent. Your repair may well bring a murderer to justice when nothing else could.”

“Yeah, well, he deserves whatever’s coming to him just for wrecking my radio. Who is the murderer by the way?”

“Maybe we should get everyone together and talk about it,” Pauline said. She looked to Mike who nodded his agreement.

“Bring Catrina and join us in the lounge, Laurent,” Pauline said, making her way back into the house.

## 35

# MISS RIDDELL EXPLAINS

THE WHOLE GROUP was gathered in the lounge. Disgruntled through lack of coffee, they stared at each other in angry confusion.

"Where's John?" Jo asked the question that everyone was thinking.

"When he found he couldn't murder me," Pauline said, "he took a snowmobile and made a run for it."

"What? When?"

"About four in the morning," Pauline said.

"Are you sure it is John?" Jo asked, looking about as though he might be hiding behind the furniture.

"I've been sure for some time," Pauline said. "I only got convincing evidence yesterday."

"How did you know it was him?" Saul asked. "He struck me as a really nice guy."

"I didn't, at first. I was as mystified as everyone," Pauline said. "After all, most people here had only a working relationship with each other and some even less than that. It seemed inconceivable there was enough hatred in the group for murder."

"Well, when did you see your way to solving the puzzle?" Mike asked.

Pauline laughed. "The moment I realized almost everyone at the lodge thought I'd done it," she replied. "It's said the thought of being hanged clarifies the mind wonderfully and the realization I was the scapegoat to be lynched, metaphorically speaking, clarified my mind. Who in this small gathering could have hated Arnie so much they'd kill him and why was it made to look like I'd done it?"

"And why was that?"

"Because the murderer had singled me out to take the blame," Pauline said. "I didn't see that right away, of course. I still thought it was just my bad luck that I'd been known to dislike Arnie and had advised Mike not to hire him. I just couldn't see any other connection between Arnie and I in the present day. I didn't realize until later it was all about the past."

"When in the past?" Tom asked. "And exactly why didn't you like Arnie? No one has really explained that to me."

Pauline frowned. "The reason we didn't like each other was because I'd been his go-to assistant on the first audit I'd done for Seaforth and Partners. I hadn't liked him as a person, and I didn't like the methods he was using to uncover some unpleasant truths in the company being audited. We were supposed to be dispassionate, neutral observers and researchers. Arnie behaved more like a vigilante hunting down wrongdoers and the methods he was using, like browbeating the man I now know was John Beresford's father, were particularly cruel."

"And that motive didn't strike you right away?" Mike asked. "Wasn't that first audit at Seaforth the first thing that came to mind?"

"Yes and no. I considered it but dismissed the thought

because no one here even knew about it – until I told Mike and he shared it with Bryan," Pauline said. "And that happened too late to have influenced the murderer, who had already killed Arnie. I thought whatever the motive, it had to be something recent."

"And Bryan's death?" Tom asked.

"It was then I wondered if I'd been the real target," Pauline said, "and that brought me back to the old audit and my involvement with Arnie. I couldn't see why, though, because no one here was involved; some are too young, some too old, and only Gilles was with Seaforth."

"Why did he try to kill you," Jo asked, "if he'd already framed you for the first murder? Murdering you would have ruined that plan."

"It was because John didn't know anything about me. Consequently, his first plan, to have me jailed for Arnie's murder, didn't consider my being asked to investigate. He thought Arnie was the guiltiest and should die; I was less so and should just live out the rest of my life in prison. When he learned I have considerable experience in investigations, he realized he couldn't wait for the law to take its course. My guess is originally he was going to *poison* Arnie and frame me as the less guilty of the two, which is why he had the poison with him. But sometime during that ski trip onto the lake, he saw my ski pole as a better solution, which meant he had the poison available to use on me when he realized his mistake."

"For a time," Mike said, "you seemed to favor the Pomerleaus as the culprits. Why was that?"

"I'd heard Catrina tell Laurent that he wasn't to do anything," Pauline said, "and she was clearly talking about a man among the guests who had in some way harmed her years before. Once again, Catrina, Laurent, and Arnie were of an age. John and Tom are too young. Mike, Gilles, and Bryan too old." She held up her hand to suppress the objections she could see Gilles and Mike about to make. "I know that in theory any one of you three could have been the person Catrina was angry with, but there was a second reason. You'd all been here to this house before. As I understood it, this was Arnie's first time here, which made him the more likely candidate. To be honest, my bias had already suggested it would be the kind of thing he'd do."

"You also suspected John because the police could find nothing on him," Mike said. "If you remember, I said at the time if he had no police record that was a good thing. You, however, remained suspicious."

Pauline nodded. "I did. There's a difference between not having a criminal record and not having a record of any kind. The storm and his cross-border past had made checking difficult, of course, but it still made me uneasy. I just couldn't see at that time what he had against Arnie and me."

"What changed your mind?"

"He did. I overheard a discussion you were all having as I returned from the garage. He said, 'I heard Arnie caused the death of someone' but I've never heard anyone say that. Have any of you?"

There were blank stares in answer to this question, which was as clear an answer as Pauline could have wished for.

"That's when you realized there was a connection between Arnie, you, and him that would explain Arnie's murder and why you were being framed?" Mike said.

"Exactly," Pauline said. "I saw that this murder hit at two people with one crime. But I still couldn't see how John was involved."

"When we got the phone back, you were able to discover... what exactly?"

"I discovered that John was right. One of the three who went to prison because of our audit was killed there. Jerry, and Renata at the Seaforth office, dug out the names of those who had suffered because of our audit," Pauline said. "You may remember, Gilles, the company we audited was declared bankrupt and three of their executives went to prison."

Gilles nodded. "I remember," he said. "It wasn't my audit, but it made quite a stir throughout our company as well as the Toronto business community."

"Arnie left Seaforth immediately after," Pauline continued. "Ed Seaforth liked what had happened as little as I did. Anyhow, I never saw Arnie again, for which I was profoundly grateful, until I discovered he was a guest this weekend."

"But lots of people go to prison and people aren't murdered over it," Mike said.

"That's true but this was more than just going to prison," Pauline said. "Inspector Ormiston discovered that one of the men, Jeffrey Pearson, was killed in prison. That seemed like a real motive for revenge."

"You mean revenge by his family?"

"Or friends or lovers," Pauline replied. "It was the only thing I'd come across in this research that suggested an emotion strong enough for murder. As it turned out, Jeffrey Pearson had a family."

"But," Gilles said, "John's name isn't Pearson."

"Which was the next hurdle to clear," Pauline replied. "The dead man's family disappeared right after his funeral and were gone from the records."

"Gone from the records," Jo exclaimed. "How could that

be? We're only talking six years ago. Records and people don't just disappear in that time."

"True," Pauline said, "unless they want to. And they wanted to, very badly. You see the son had inherited his father's knack for figures. John was going to study finance at university and become an accountant. Who would hire the son of an accountant who'd been jailed for fraud?"

"It makes sense," Mike said. "We certainly wouldn't anyhow. I know we shouldn't judge kids by their parents, but we deal with sensitive information. We couldn't risk it."

Pauline nodded. "Exactly," she said. "Mrs. Pearson returned to the States and reverted to using her maiden name of Beresford for herself and John. John finished his education and training down there. He returned here when he was offered a position. I don't know if he always intended to hunt down and punish Arnie and me but when this opportunity came along, he took it."

"You think he only came back to Canada for revenge?"

"Perhaps not only," Pauline said thoughtfully, "but it was in his mind, I think. After all, his qualifications were American, and he could earn more down there than here. I think his father's death set him on the road to murder. It may have only started as fantasies of bringing justice to those he saw as having caused the death of his father but, over time, those fantasies became plans and then he set out to deliver what he saw as natural justice."

"He must be mad," Gilles said. "You and Arnie may have exposed his father but there was a trial and a defense. And he wasn't killed by the law but by some violent felon. That could have happened on the street."

"People love the idea of bringing justice down on those who have wronged them," Pauline said. "There are comics, TV programs, and movies devoted to nothing but that. It would be easy for an angry young man to think he was doing good work in punishing those who had started this chain of horror."

"His father did that when he embezzled all those funds," Gilles said.

"I know that," Pauline said, "but he clearly thought the stealing they did was a victimless crime and what we did put his father in harm's way, which is true. I'm not defending him, just explaining what I think happened and why an otherwise sensible young man could persuade himself do such an awful thing."

"Maybe it's as simple as criminality runs in that family," Gilles said, shrugging. "I don't much care about motivation, good or bad. It's what people do that counts and a crime is a crime so far as I'm concerned."

"I have a lot of sympathy with that view too sometimes," Pauline said. "Arnie wasn't a nice man, but he didn't deserve what happened to him and Bryan by all accounts was a good man who definitely shouldn't have been killed."

"It's still an extreme reaction to what had happened to his father," Jo said, puzzled.

Pauline nodded. "His fantasies might have stayed just fantasies but then his mother died. I suspect that's what tipped him over the edge."

"I hope they catch him," Saul said. "I liked old Bryan."

Mike nodded. "Amen to that."

Saul cleared his throat. "Pauline, I owe you an apology. In my defense, I should say I really did believe you to be guilty. However, it wasn't sufficient excuse for all I've said and thought these past days."

Pauline smiled. "I understood your feelings completely and could therefore sympathize with your behavior."

"I'm sorry too," Tom said. "This has been an education. I'll be more wary in future."

"Me too, Pauline," Jo said.

"I wish we knew if they had him," Gilles said, diplomatically changing the subject.

"I'll call them again," Pauline said. "I would think he'd have arrived at the road long ago."

As she left the house and entered the garage, she heard the roar of snowmobile engines and thinking it was LaPlante, she opened the garage's outer door. However, the line of snowmobiles that was passing along the road, having come up from the lake, were clearly not police. Disappointed, Pauline watched them disappear along the road, leaving only the fading roar and a faint scent of exhaust in the clean, still morning air.

After speaking on the radio with the police operator, she returned to the others, who were now happily making, and laughing at, awkward jokes. Pauline knew it would be some time before they were comfortable with themselves and each other.

"Well?" Mike demanded, when she entered the room.

Pauline shook her head. "They think he turned off along one of the firebreak trails. They were at the junction quickly enough, so they feel certain he didn't go that way."

"He can't get far," Gilles said.

"They need to find him though," Pauline said. "He could freeze to death if he runs out of gas in the forest."

"No great loss if he does," Jo said.

The sound of other snowmobiles could be heard outside. Pauline said, "The fine weather has everyone out on their toys. With luck someone will rescue John before nightfall."

"We should get outside for some fresh air and sunshine

too," Mike said heartily, "before the police arrive and keep us all indoors making statements."

Gilles picked up this suggestion, "You're right. After all, that's why we're here."

"I'm not going anywhere," Jo said.

"Well, I shall," Pauline said, cheerfully. "We've all been prisoners here in the lodge for days. Some fresh air will do me the world of good." Finishing her toast, Pauline headed out to the mud room.

Tom joined her as she was doing the final fastenings of her ski suit. "I'll join you," he said.

"I'll wait outside," Pauline replied, lifting a pair of snowshoes off the rack. "I've never done this before," she said, waving the snowshoes. "Learning a new skill will take my mind off everything."

Outside, she found snowshoes weren't as easy to fit as cross-country skis and she was still fiddling with them when Tom arrived, also with snowshoes.

"Let me," he said, kneeling in the snow to adjust the bindings. When he was done, he quickly fixed his own.

"Where to?" Tom asked.

"The lake," Pauline said. "I won't trip over roots, branches, and boulders out there."

"Okay," Tom said. "Should I lead? That way you can see the action that works with them. It's a lot different to cross-country skiing. Using snowshoes, well, requires some practice."

"Sounds like a plan," Pauline said. She watched him lift and lower each foot and did her best to copy the motion. Snowshoes, she discovered, were heavier and even more ungainly than skis. And constantly lifting them was physically tiring, unlike skis that just slid along the surface. The downhill trail to the lake also proved awkward and she almost fell more than once. Out on the flat surface of the lake, however, was a different story and she quickly got into the rhythm.

When they'd gone a quarter of a mile along the shoreline, Pauline called a halt. "I need a rest," she said.

Tom stopped and together they admired the wintry view. The vast plain of snow on the frozen lake gave way at the edges to dark, snow-covered trees. Smoke rose lazily upward from chimneys of cottages where people were staying but otherwise nothing marred the serene ice-blue sky.

"It is beautiful here," Pauline said softly, more to herself than to her companion.

Tom nodded. "If you're warm and dry and if you have a heated home and plenty of food, then yes, it is. Otherwise, it's deadly."

Pauline nodded. "I'm always glad I didn't come here as a settler."

Tom laughed. "My parents spend the winter in Florida every year," he said. "They have a summer business that they close after Thanksgiving. They don't come back until May the next year. For them, it's always summer."

"We owe so much to planes, trains, and cars," Pauline said. "This land in winter lifts my soul but, one day, if I'm still here in Canada when I retire, I'll probably do as your parents do."

They set off, turning toward Mike's lodge, and saw Gilles and Saul emerge from the road, their downhill momentum sending their skis skimming gently over the snow. With a wave, the skiers headed out across the lake. Pauline and Tom continued stepping their way back.

At the foot of the hill, Pauline said, "You go ahead. I must rest before I attempt that." She pointed at the gentle slope up to the lodge.

"Take the snowshoes off and walk," Tom said. "We did a lot for a first day."

Pauline shook her head. "I'll finish as I started, thanks. Don't wait, I won't be long. I'll take five minutes to refresh my legs and I'll follow you."

"Okay, but if you aren't inside in fifteen minutes, I'll be back to carry you inside."

Pauline laughed. "Very gallant. If I'm not back in fifteen minutes, it's because I can't make it up the hill and I'll expect you to make good on your promise."

She watched him trot easily up the hill and turn, disappearing behind the buildings around the lodge's parking area.

# 36

# THE WHY

Across the lake, she could see the two skiers and others who must have come out from cottages. The sound of engines told her there were snowmobiles or all-terrain quad bikes about. They didn't disturb the serenity of the scene as she'd thought they would. They also didn't disturb her own quiet. At least, not as much as a movement she could see among the firs at the farther edge of the road did. She watched snow sliding off branches as whatever it was drew nearer. *What do you do if you meet a bear?*

The bushes parted and John stepped out, brushing the snow from his clothes.

"You came back," Pauline said. "I hoped you would." He wasn't startled, she noticed. He'd been waiting to meet her alone. It was frightening he'd appeared when she was stuck in her snowshoes, though. No flight for her. If he'd come to finish his mission, fight was her only choice, and her Beretta was in her room.

"Then it was stupid to hang out here with no one to save you."

"I also thought it likely you just wanted to explain,"

Pauline said.

He nodded. “I didn’t know you’d tried to stop Hamilton.”

“Until after you’d poisoned the breadbasket and Bryan died,” Pauline said.

“Yes. I thought you were his junior partner in crime,” John said, approaching her slowly.

“I’d be more comfortable if you kept your distance.”

He stopped. “It wasn’t right what he did. Dad wasn’t a bad man and Hamilton got him killed,” John said.

“I remember your father well,” Pauline told him. “Unfortunately, he’d allowed himself to be hustled along a path that was wrong until it was too late for him to turn back, as so many of us do.”

“People shouldn’t be killed for something that could hardly be called a crime,” John said.

Pauline nodded. “Skimming off the rounding error in financial transactions may seem harmless but it made them and those behind them a lot of money.”

“And injured no one,” John cried. “The money didn’t really exist, except in computer systems. In the real world, there are dollars and cents; everything beyond a cent isn’t a coin. It isn’t money. How can you steal something that doesn’t exist?”

“Computers have certainly brought us a whole new class of crimes,” Pauline agreed. “And I’m not sure they’ll ever deliver anything good in return.”

“Exactly,” said John eagerly. “I knew you’d understand.”

“I understand,” Pauline said, “but I can’t approve. Those fractions of a cent, multiplied over millions of currency transactions, made your father and his accomplices wealthy and the people behind his two accomplices even richer. They were old-fashioned gangsters, though I’m sure they wore nice suits.”

"Dad told me he never intended any of it," John said. "He was bullied into it by the other two. They weren't accomplices, they were enforcers."

"They were probably in fear of their lives as well," Pauline said.

"Then your accomplice Hamilton bullied Dad into admitting what they'd done."

"As I said, your father wasn't cut out for a life of crime," Pauline replied. "He was too easy-going to push back against his two colleagues, too weak to push back against Hamilton, and then easy pickings for the police. They soon had him point them at the shady people behind it all. Your father never stood a chance from that moment on."

"If Hamilton had just made a report," John said. "Left it that..."

"It wouldn't have saved him, John. Your father's nature was too yielding, too easy to bully. They would have wanted more and more from him and one day, would have disposed of him because he was the weakest link in their chain."

"He was one of the first to see the possibilities of computers in finance, you know," John said, wistfully.

Pauline nodded. "Agreed. His skills were programming and accounting, not fighting with thuggish criminals."

"If you'd pushed harder against Hamilton's bullying...," John began. He stopped when Pauline shook her head.

"It wouldn't have changed the outcome," she said. "Our report would still have exposed the wrongdoing; their company board would have begun a police investigation and your father would have cracked. He was a good man who got in with truly bad people and way out of his depth."

John nodded. "I'm not sorry about Hamilton," he said. "He got what he deserved."

"I can't agree, John, but you need to give yourself up when the police arrive. We don't need any more deaths."

"Mom died," he said. "Did you know?"

Pauline nodded. "The police told me. I'm sorry."

"It was cancer," John said. "That's what was on the death certificate. Only I know it was a broken heart."

"You need a positive spirit to fight cancer," Pauline agreed.

"She didn't fight at all. It was diagnosed, they started treatment, and she died. So quick. I decided right there at her funeral, I would find the people who did this to my family and avenge my parents' deaths."

"Is that where you learned about curare?"

"It's where the idea solidified," John said. "I knew about it from National Geographic documentaries I watched as a kid. Having the doctor tell us they would be using it to help mom during her surgery seemed like the final piece in the puzzle."

Pauline nodded. "You stole it from the hospital down there?"

"It was easy," John said. "Hospitals always have people wandering around in them that staff don't know."

"But it isn't poisonous in the dosage hospitals use."

John laughed. "As I'd learned from Geographic, the South American tribes boil down the sap until it's strong enough to kill. I just gently warmed what I stole until it was a soft paste. You can learn so much from TV."

"That's where you learned curare has to go straight into the bloodstream."

He nodded. "I was puzzled for a time how I could inject you and Arnie. In the end, I injected him," he grinned, "but without the poison. It meant I had more for the others."

"And the breadbasket?"

"When you begin planning deaths," John replied, "you see so many possibilities. It came to me the moment I saw the fancy artwork on the basket. I just untwisted it as I stood there waiting for the toaster to pop."

"You took quite a chance, though," Pauline said, hoping if she could keep him talking long enough sooner or later someone would come looking for her.

"They were all sitting around the table," he replied. "Even if they looked at me they would only see my back. They couldn't see what I was doing with my hands. And even if someone came beside me, I'd have just said the metalwork was loose and I was putting it back in place."

Pauline nodded. "I can see how that would be. Still, getting the curarine onto the spike might have raised suspicions."

"It might but it didn't. I took the vial from my pocket, opened it and slipped the vial over the spike and coated the metal well. It was all done in seconds."

"Yes, I see," Pauline said. She paused and then continued, "I know Bryan was a mistake, John, but even Arnie Hamilton played only a small part in what happened to your father."

He smiled grimly. "Maybe, but he was the first to walk into my sights. I'd have found the others eventually. Now I won't."

Pauline thought it more likely that the people who killed his father would kill him too, once the story came out and he was in prison.

A clattering roar sounded in the sky and in a moment a helicopter circled and descended onto the lake, the blast from its rotors swirling the snow into mini tornadoes that danced across the lake before collapsing.

Pauline watched John. If he was going to kill her this was

his final chance. She desperately needed to keep him distracted as the police arrived.

"You can't say Bryan deserved to die, though, John. That's harder to accept."

He nodded. "I imagine all people who demand justice find they've punished the wrong person sometimes," he said sadly. "I don't know how they live with it. I know I'll never forgive myself for Bryan's death. Even if it had been you, as it was meant to be, it would still have been wrong, as I discovered later."

"Tell them what you've told me, John. The law isn't entirely without compassion."

"You tell them," he said. "I'll wait inside." He turned and began walking up the road toward the house.

Pauline shuffled her feet and snowshoes so she could watch both John and the man approaching, who she took to be Inspector LaPlante. She smiled at him in greeting, "Inspector LaPlante, I presume. I'm Pauline Riddell." She held out her hand in greeting.

Before LaPlante was able to take her hand, Pauline saw, from the corner of her eye, John fling his fist up to his neck and throw back his head. Then he cast aside a small glass bottle.

"You're too late, Inspector," she said. "The murderer has just escaped."

He followed her gaze and watched as John's confident stride hesitated, slowed, and then stopped. For a moment, he stood upright. Then he fell to the ground as if poleaxed.

"He still had the rest of the poison," Pauline said. "He's just injected himself with it."

"You're sure it was him?"

"Yes, but you must do your own investigation, Inspector."

## 37

## ONE MONTH LATER

"Can we talk, Pauline?" Mike said, poking his head through the door of her office.

Pauline smiled. "You're the boss," she replied.

He entered and closed the door behind him. "I've just been meeting with Saul and Jo," he said, seating himself in her guest chair. "What do you think they told me?"

"That they were leaving to start their own firm?" Pauline guessed.

"You knew?" He sounded angry.

"I didn't but after that weekend, I thought they might," Pauline said. "Hiring me had already made them discontented. That weekend, when you took my part over them was the final straw, I think."

He grimaced. "They both wanted more than their performance warranted," he said. "In a few years, they may have grown into the next level but not right now and it's right now we have the need."

"You must have a woman on the board," Pauline said.

He nodded. "The pressure is becoming unbearable."

"It's wrong," Pauline said.

He laughed. "Perhaps, but will you take it?"

Pauline smiled. "When I asked John if he'd join Neufeldt if asked, he said *we all love to be wanted*. He was right. Yes, I'll take the position."

"I'll set the process in motion," Mike said. He paused. "I'm not sure I ever said thank you, though I'm sure you must know how grateful I am you brought the murders of Arnie and Bryan to a peaceful close."

"I'm glad I could," Pauline said. "I'm sorry there was no way of saving John, though. Still, in the end, his way was for the best."

"You knew he still had poison left?"

"I thought it likely," Pauline said, "and if he no longer wanted to kill me, he had to put himself out of the reach of the law and the people who killed his father."

Mike nodded. "As you say, for the best."

When Mike was gone, Pauline pushed her chair back and went to the window, looking out on the city where springtime was showing in the nearby park and trees. A new adventure, she thought. *One that will require more of me than investigating murders.*

It would require political savvy, and she hated politics and politicians. That she'd gotten from Inspector Ramsay all those years ago. On many occasions she'd thought, and said, 'I look forward to the day when politics is recognized as a mental illness and those who wish to pursue it, professional or amateur, are kept away from all positions of authority.' Now she was joining the ranks of the amateur politicians. Was she ready for that? Only time would tell.

* * *

IF YOU ENJOYED THIS BOOK, please leave a review on Amazon. You can find it here: The Dead of Winter

## NEWSLETTER INVITATION

To be kept up-to-date with future Miss Riddell's Cozy Mysteries, sign up for my newsletter:

https://bit.ly/PCJAmesNewsletter

Or if you prefer a QR Code:

## BONUS CONTENT

This next story begins where ***Then There Were... Two Murders?*** ended.

Here's where you can pre-order THE PAST NEVER DIES

Chapter 1: Northumberland, England, January 1954

"Here he is," Poppy said, seeing Ramsay making his way into the Snug. "You're late, Inspector. We're a drink ahead of you. You'll have to buy us a second when you buy yours."

Ramsay smiled. "What are you having?" he asked.

He returned a few minutes later with the drinks on a tray.

"It's ungentlemanly to keep a lady waiting," Poppy said. "Keeping two waiting is unforgivable."

"Unfortunately, something came up at work and I had to stay and set the team in motion," he said. "Cheers!" He lifted his glass and they responded.

"Anything in my line, Inspector?" Poppy asked eagerly.

Ramsay shook his head. "Not yet," he said, "but there maybe something for Miss Riddell to ponder."

"Why can't the press be told?" Poppy demanded.

"There's no story," Ramsay said. "It's just a small matter I'd like an outside opinion on, that's all."

"And you think I can help, Inspector?" Pauline asked, puzzled. "Tell me."

"Later, Miss Riddell," Ramsay said. "Today we're celebrating your success in solving those two murders."

Pauline flushed pink and Ramsay laughed.

"You're blushing, Pauline," Poppy teased her.

"I'm not used to having my praises quite so publicly sung," Pauline said.

"Then we'll never mention them again," Ramsay teased her. "That way you'll know how highly you're regarded."

"To Pauline," Poppy said, raising her glass. "Our very own Miss Marple."

As they left pub, Ramsay took the opportunity of Poppy's absence to say, "Please phone me at this number, Miss Riddell." He handed her a page torn from a notepad. "It's my home phone because I'd like to talk privately."

"What is this about, Inspector," Pauline asked, faintly concerned she was getting in above her head.

"Later, Miss Riddell," he replied. "It isn't a murder, not even a death."

Poppy joined them outside, looking at each of them searchingly trying to guess what they'd been saying without her.

"I must go," Ramsay said. "Good night to you both. I'm sure we'll meet again."

Pauline and Poppy walked back to Poppy's flat with Poppy questioning Pauline every step of the way.

"Enough, Poppy," Pauline said, when they'd reached her car. "Inspector Ramsay hasn't told me anything and even if he had, I wouldn't break his confidence. Thank you for these newspaper clippings," she took them from her bag and put them in the car. "I'll treasure them. The high point and end of my career as a sleuth."

"Nonsense," Poppy said. "He's already asking for more help. You're going places my girl, whether you like it or not."

Pauline laughed. "I'd be a real Jonah if even more murders were to come anywhere near me, wouldn't I? See you soon, Poppy." She leapt in her car and drove away, wondering how she could show the Bertrams the newspaper stories without appearing to boast about them. She decided it would be best just to show them and not worry about appearances.

## ALSO BY P.C. JAMES

The whole Miss Riddell series can be found here.

Or here: https://www.amazon.com/dp/B08MQXFRK7

For someone who prefers **large print**: In The Beginning, There Was a Murder

For someone who prefers listening to books, ***In the Beginning, There Was a Murder*** is now available as an audiobook on Amazon and here on Audible.

GoodReads: https://www.goodreads.com/author/show/20856827.P_C_James

More books by the author can be found here.

Or here:
https://www.amazon.com/dp/B08MQXFRK7~/e/B01DFGG2U2

# ABOUT THE AUTHOR: P.C. JAMES

P.C. James is the author of the popular Miss Riddell series of cozy mysteries and this is the eighth published book in the series.

He always loved mysteries, especially those involving Agatha Christie's Miss Marple. Perhaps because Miss Marple reminded him of his aunts when he was growing up. But Christie never told us much about Miss Marple's earlier life. When writing his own elderly super-sleuth series, James is tracing her career from the start.

After retiring, P.C. James became a writer and, as a writer, spends much of his day feverishly typing or doing one of the many others tasks authoring requires. For the rest, you'll find him running, cycling, walking, and taking wildlife photos wherever and whenever he can. His cozy mystery series begins in northern England because that was his home growing up and England is also the home of so many great cozy mysteries. However, Miss Riddell loves to travel as much as the author does, and the stories will take us to many different places around the world.

Printed in Great Britain
by Amazon

80047057R00130